Virgin Islands

Virgin Islands

A Serialized Novel by
Wesley Adams and Daphne McGee

Book 9 of the Soap Opera Inspired Story Collection
Series Created by Gary Brin

Episodes 1-7

In memory of Bob the Cat who tragically passed away in June 2020 during the writing of this novel. He was immortalized in the bestselling 2012 memoir *A Street Cat Named Bob* as well as the 2016 movie of the same name of which he played himself. Bob the Cat is credited with saving a drug-addicted homeless man from taking his own life—resulting in worldwide fame upon the publication of the above-mentioned book.

In memory of Niels Mortensen (1966-1999) of whom the character Niels Anderssen is based upon.

Contents

Intro

The backdrop used for *Virgin Islands* is set in and around various locations in the United States Virgin Islands, specifically the island of St. Thomas. The nearby island of Puerto Rico also figured into the plotline when needed in order to enhance the storyline. Like previous novels in the Soap Opera Inspired Story Collection, the story exists only in the pages of the series and not reality. However, like previous novels in this series many of the locations mentioned are real and do exist. With the exception of bookstores, cafes and selected homes—as well as Mysterious Island—all other geographic locations used as backdrops for the story are real and can be easily found by using Google. As with other published titles in the Soap Opera Inspired Story Collection Series—characters from existing books will make appearances as part of the continuing storyline to untangle previous plotlines.

In the "ripped from the headlines" scenario, many of the events used for storyline purposes are taken from real-life events that were reworked into a fictional setting. Nevertheless *Virgin Islands* was specifically written to resemble traditional classic soap operas of the past to a certain extent—and was written with the intention that it's playing to a visual audience and therefore will emulate a scripted format rather than the usual storytelling methods displayed in popular full-length modern novels such as *Yacht People* by Mary-Rose Hayes and *Memory of Eva Ryker* by Donald Stanwood. It should also be noted that each episode of this series were written in a brief span of 6-12 days or less and therefore shouldn't be confused with being great literature. The goal of this serialized series of books was simply to mimic episodes of prime-time soaps—by creating visual entertainment on a printed page—and not to create a literary masterpiece.

Virgin Islands takes place approximately at the same time the events in *Marble Hills* are occurring in New England. Some characters from previous novels in the Soap Opera Inspired Story Collection Series are featured throughout this book as part of the present story in order to resolve previous unfinished stories.

Gary Brin
Series Creator

In an effort to have an accurate portrayal of the dialogue used for the *Soap Opera Inspired Story Collection Series* people were anonymously observed in shopping malls, schools, places of employment, and on public streets in order to capture a definitive portrayal of how people of various ages and cultures interacted and talked to each other when they thought no one was listening. While some select dialogue was exaggerated for dramatic purposes when needed—the manner and tone of which people were observed speaking to each other in casual and private conversations is accurate. Exact wording was not copied verbatim for the most part, but the way certain types of topics and conversations are addressed by characters in this serialized series is based on actual situations that were observed over a period of several dozen years.

Prologue

1
Sixteen Years Earlier

A teenage boy grabs a frightened girl and slaps her around as he seems to get a perverse thrill from his actions. The girl begins to cry as she falls against a bookcase several feet away.

"Did you think I'd allow it?"

He grabs her again.

"Did you think I wouldn't find out?"

He hits her across her face in an angry rage while she seems to cower as she retreats into a ball. He begins laughing.

"Your lover boy is gonna pay."

He makes a slashing motion with his hand.

"I'll teach him a lesson—one he'll never forget."

He clenches his fist.

"Then you and I will talk."

He watches her reaction and begins laughing.

"No one is gonna help you—no one at all—you've got no one but me—and don't you ever forget it—I own you."

The girl tries to stand. He points his finger at her as he reaches into his pocket and pulls out a pair of brass knuckles.

"I think you need a few lessons on obeying me—got to make sure you know who's boss—who calls the shots."

Seconds later he begins hitting her as screams echo loudly throughout the tiny bedroom amid his loud laughter.

2

The teenage boy looks at the girl lying on the floor. Her legs are smeared with semen as he stands up. He glances at his penis and laughs loudly—he points at her again and grins.

"It's you and me all the way—that punk is no longer going to try to get into your pants—that I guarantee—he's toast."

He smiles broadly as he looks at his penis again.

"Uh-huh—I intend to make frequent visits—sample your wares until I decide your future—take what is rightfully mine."

He begins laughing as he mockingly points at her.

"You and I are bound at the hip now—no one will be closer than the two of us—especially not that stuck-up geeky loser."

He makes a lewd gesture with his finger.

"I think I'm going to pay him a friendly visit."

The girl begins sobbing as he zips his pants and walks to the door. He stops and faces her again. He winks at her.

"I hear he has a job at the diner on the corner of Fourth Street and Monroe. I know for a fact the parking lot in the back of the diner has plenty of places for a guy like me to hide—and wait patiently for just the right moment—to even the score."

He makes a slashing gesture with his hand.

3

The parking lot is empty as shadows of the night begin to creep about as a teenage boy comes into the lot. He stops a few times as if worried about the eerie stillness permeating the area. He reaches into his jacket pocket for his keys. As they jingle he seems to feel better as the noise interrupts the silence. He begins walking again as he whistles briefly before stopping again.

"Got to remind management to replace the lights for the lot pronto—would make things easier to see in the dark."

He turns around suddenly as he hears a rustling noise. He sees several rats scurry away and reacts. He shakes his head.

"Damn those fiends—even the alley cats are afraid to confront them—too bad snakes are hard to come by around here—slimy suckers would easily gobble those things up."

There is another noise several feet away. He turns around just as a fist smashes into his face. He yells out in fright as several more pummeling blows fall on him. He screams for help.

"No one is gonna help you lover boy."

The teenage boy is hit again and again by his much bigger rival until he's a bloody mess lying on the pavement. He watches as his attacker grins broadly while he stands over him. Mocking laughter echoes as he realizes what is about to take place.

"Say goodnight sweet prince."

A foot comes down with force on his neck as he gasps for air while he's struck again and again until he finally stops begging for mercy. Seconds later his attacker calmly walks away.

4

"Your lover boy is no more. He got what he deserved and now I think it's time you realize I own you—body and soul."

He laughs as he grabs the girl by her hair.

"Don't you ever defy me again—I won't tolerate it."

He hits her hard across the face as she cries out in pain while her terrified eyes react with each aggressive attack.

"I'm the only one you'll have between your legs from now on—the only one you'll allow to plow you—is that clear?"

He begins laughing gleefully.

Page **15**

A Brief Look at the First Episode

Secrets from the past begin to unravel as a man plots diabolical revenge against his ex with help from his clueless sister—as a rich family faces events from their past that threatens to destroy the perfect image they've created over the last two decades—while a famous writer comes back to the islands for a book signing.

Episode 1
Gameplay Blues

1
Magens Bay Beach
St. Thomas
United States Virgin Islands
Present Day

"I don't see why I have to pretend?"

Savannah Windsor turns around to face Brent Crawford as he shoots her a warning glance. He angrily clenches his fist.

"I already told you why you have to keep my name from coming up when you talk about your past—my ex is not a fool by any means—if she even suspects—we're already sunk."

He runs his fingers through his hair.

"I've waited a long time to stick it to that miserable bitch for how she treated me—dumped me like used trash."

"Why happened between you two anyway?"

Brent turns to look out at the beach several feet away and seems irritated by his sister asking him stupid questions.

"She played me—then threw me away."

He pounds his fist on the steering wheel and sighs.

"Astrid Blakely is seriously loaded—has more money than God since she cleverly swindled some stupid old fool from Maine who killed himself several years back amid a scandalous outing of his nefarious activities played out by one of his former lovers."

Brent makes a lewd gesture with his hand.

"She owes me—that bitch is gonna pay dearly."

He clenches his fist again.

"I'll ruin her if it's the last thing I do."

Savannah seems worried as she looks at her brother.

"What if she calls the cops on us?"

Brent waves his hand in the air and smirks.

"She can't call the cops if she doesn't know she's being played by yours truly. She'll never see it coming—then wham—a few carefully played situations and she'll wish she'd never crossed me. She'll beg for mercy—she'll cry for help—guaranteed."

Savannah watches as Brent begins laughing.

2

Back Street Cafe

"Are you sure this is a good idea?"

Boris Birney watches as John Smythe grins and nods several times as he turns to look at the computer screen again.

"Uh-huh, I'm sure, come on, it'll be fun. You, me, and our girlfriends for a day trip to Mysterious Island. It's been opened for a year now—there's nothing to worry about. They turned it into a park right after the press went away. We've been invited to take a tour by Zimmerman. He insisted by the way—said he was paying for it—the ferry, food, the works. Don't wimp out on me now."

Boris shakes his head several times.

"You're a magnet for trouble Smythe."

John grins broadly.

"Uh-huh—but without me you'd be living a really dull life right about now, slaving away in some office job where everyone spends their free time minding other people's business."

Boris runs his fingers through his hair and sighs loudly.

Page 18

"Fine—whatever—but if anything happens to me or Alison I'm holding you personally responsible—no exceptions."

John gleefully rolls his eyes.

"There isn't going to be any drama—what could happen on an island that has security guards patrolling the grounds from dawn to dusk? Nothing—except of course if those two dead guys show up—and their creepy old grandfather—what was his name? Oh, that's right? Zaroff—Count Zaroff if I recall. Dude was a piece of work from what I read in the *Times* review yesterday."

Boris gives John a knowing look.

"Sandra King is coming to the islands to sign her book at a bookstore in Havensight Mall. Heard they ordered a thousand copies in case there was a huge crowd wanting a copy—book has been selling on Amazon for the past two months. I think Warner Brothers optioned it for a movie already—or a miniseries—I forgot which—I saw her on CNN talking about it last week."

John wags his finger at Boris.

"I bet you already bought a copy."

Boris takes a swig of his drink and grins.

"Hey, I'm mentioned in the book a few times—of course I bought a copy—it's not every day you see your name in print."

John rolls his eyes and jabs Boris.

"If it hadn't been for me it would never have happened at all. I saved the day—and don't you forget it—like ever."

Boris makes a fist and shakes it.

"Can your ego get any bigger John—it always has to be about you—never can let anyone shine for even a moment."

John grins broadly and gestures.

3
Stumpy Bay Beach

A couple is nimbly walking along a dirt road leading to the beach. Most of the road has huge portions of the surfacing missing due to water runoff from the nearby ravines. They stop and slowly look around. The area seems completely deserted.

"How much longer until we get to the beach—my feet are killing me—could use a drink of water right about now."

Alexis de Hoya gives his girlfriend a knowing look and wipes sweat from his brow. He peers through the trees.

"It's just down the ways from here, Marisa. According to Marco you can see the beach just past those trees at the end of the rocky cropping. He comes here all the time to scuba dive."

Marisa Rossmore puts her hands on her hips.

"Uh-huh—like Marco Verde knows anything about good directions—I haven't forgotten what happened last month."

Alexis begins laughing and gestures.

"OK—OK—my cousin has problems with direction—but this time he's right about the beach being nearby just over that next curve in the road. I can hear the surf from here. Listen."

Marisa turns toward where Alexis is pointing.

"I don't hear anything."

Alexis rolls his eyes and gestures at Marisa again.

"Let's just keep going—Stumpy Beach is gonna be worth it. Marco said the place is always deserted. No one visits."

Marisa shakes her fist at Alexis.

"What if there's some hermit living there—just waiting for us to come by—come by so he can slash our throats with a machete or something—drink our blood just for kicks."

Alexis takes Marisa's hand.

"Come on—I'll protect you. But just for the record you've got to stop watching those old movies from the 1980s where stupid teenagers were being chased by some deranged dude with mommy issues—there's no one here—no one except us."

He grins seeing her odd reaction to his comment and makes a slashing gesture with his finger. She grimaces.

"I'll never forgive you if I get killed."

Alexis makes a slashing gesture with his finger again.

"Uh-huh—I think you would."

Marisa gives Alexis a weird look and follows him until they come to the entrance. For several seconds they stare in awe at the pristine-looking beach several yards in front of them.

Armand Bell opens his eyes and looks out as the sun shines through the window of his bedroom. He sighs loudly.

"Is it morning already?"

He rubs his eyes and looks over at his girlfriend lying next to him. She opens her eyes slowly as he shakes her. She yawns as he climbs out of bed and grabs his robe. He sighs again.

"When is your mother due back?"

Armand turns to face Lily Van Tassel and grins.

"Next week—doesn't matter though—she never comes to the guest house anymore—she knows better after last year."

Lily gives Armand a knowing look.

"Oh, is that so. Did she catch you with my sister?"

Armand grins broadly.

"She caught me with her friend from college."

Lily seems disgusted.

"You slept with an old lady?"

Armand wags his finger at Lily.

"Maggie Blanding is not an old woman—she's forty."

He licks his lips several times.

"She knows things."

Lily climbs out of bed.

"Ugh—it's bad enough you slept with my sister—but some woman who is old enough to be my mother? Ugh—gross."

Armand grabs a pair of jeans lying on the floor and begins dressing as Lily combs her hair. She pauses and sighs.

"What about you and Jasmine?"

Armand turns around and faces Lily.

"What about her?"

Lily angrily shakes the hairbrush at Armand.

"Are you and her still an item?"

Armand seems annoyed and shrugs.

"Jasmine and I just friends—like relax already."

Lily walks over to Armand. She seems ready for a fight.

"I won't tolerate you skipping out on me."

Armand laughs and turns away.

"I'm not sleeping with Jasmine—but we do have a son together—what am I supposed to do—not talk to her when I go visit Trevor? You need to chill—stop expecting the worse of me every time you see me with some chick—enough already."

Lily grabs Armand by the arm.

"You really hurt me when you slept with my sister. She and I are not talking by the way—courtesy of your behavior."

Armand pulls away from Lily and laughs.

"I already told you it meant nothing—I was drunk—she was drunk—it happened—like seriously, get over it already."

Lily grabs Armand's hand again.

"You got her pregnant."

Armand jerks free of Lily's grip.

"She lost the baby—what's your problem?"

Lily walks back toward the mirror.

"If I catch you with some other girl I won't be responsible for what I do—you've been warned. I play hard—really dirty."

Armand gives Lily an odd look.

"I won't be threatened by my jealous girlfriend."

Lily throws her hairbrush at Armand.

"I'm warning you."

He begins laughing.

5
Mafolie

A car is driving along a tree-lined road with picturesque views of the city of Charlotte Amalie below. The car slows at a curve as several oncoming cars seem not to slow down.

"This view is spectacular—I bet the houses around here costs plenty—probably as much as a pad in Beverly Hills."

Justin Manslow seems irritated as he wipes sweat from his brow and grabs his cell phone. He resumes driving and grins.

Page **22**

"I hope Sandra and her new hubby arrived safely. Got to make sure nothing goes wrong. Too much money riding on her book selling a million copies before the end of next month."

He begins dialing and as the phone is picked up he pulls over by the side of the road in front of Mafolie Hotel.

"Yeah, uh-huh, it's me. I gather you and Scott made it to the hotel already? That's right—it's quite classy no doubt."

He snickers and waves his hand in the air.

"I'm right outside actually."

He laughs again and looks at the entrance of the hotel just a few yards away. He grins broadly and shuts off his cell phone.

6
Hoya Coffee Corporate Offices
Puerto Rico

"I'm through waiting Gavin. Time is money. My money to be exact—I want you here on the next flight from Miami."

Milo Wiley wipes sweat from his brow as he faces his cousin Alexander de Hoya. He grimaces and then sighs.

"It seems Gavin missed his flight."

Alexander seems irritated and shrugs.

"Likely story—that man is more trouble than he's worth to us—spends more time on his damn back than he works."

Milo leans back in his chair.

"Maybe we should start looking for his replacement just in case—someone with a better worth ethic—and married."

Alexander snickers.

"Hopefully happily married as a rule—no drama to speak of—no girlfriend on the side—or boyfriend for that matter."

Milo wags his finger at Alexander.

"My mother thought Cashe Bishoff was straight when she married him—seemed so anyway—until my sister caught him in bed with the butler—a day after the frigging wedding—sick."

He walks over to the window.

"I heard he moved back to New York."

Page **23**

Milo turns around to face Alexander and grimaces.

"My mother has never picked the right guy. She always thinks she's getting a diamond—but he turns to coal right after."

Alexander stands and walks over to his cousin.

"How is your mother anyway? I haven't heard from her in the last two weeks or so. Is she back from Monaco yet? I assume she and **Princess Stephanie** had a lot to gossip about?"

"She's in St. Thomas as we speak—staying at her usual suite at Frenchman's Reef. Apparently, one of the people who were with her on that wretched island has written a tell-all memoir on what happened. Mother said she wanted to say hi in person when we talked earlier. I assume she'll be back in San Juan in about a week or so from what she stated when I inquired."

He glances at his cell phone.

"How is Alexis handling the divorce? Is he still angry at you for calling it quits with Ingrid? From what I recall he was pretty bummed out when he caught you in bed with Celia Kwon."

Alexander runs his fingers through his hair and sighs.

7
Stumpy Bay Beach

"See, I told you it was worth it. This beach is heaven—just the two of us and nature. No pesky people to fuck anything up like always happens when you go to Magens. That place is a magnet for muscle-headed jerks who think they're God's gift to women—compensating for having a tiny pea for a brain."

Alexis puts his arms around Marisa.

"I wonder if this beach is for sale—I'd buy it without even thinking twice—pave the road and build a huge mansion."

Marisa begins laughing.

"Your family won't buy you a beach?"

Alexis grins broadly.

"Says who?"

Marisa turns to face Alexis.

"Didn't you say your old man was a tightwad?"

Alexis rolls his eyes and sighs loudly.

"Uh-huh—he's a cheap motherfucker tightwad without a doubt—but I could play the guilt card. After all, it was me that caught him in bed with his trashy assistant—busted him."

He stands up and looks around.

"I'm still mad at him if you must know. He cheated on my mother with that fucking whore. Said it didn't mean anything afterwards. Tried playing me for a fool—but I showed him—got on the phone and told mom what I'd seen. Marriage was kaput within an hour. Mom rented a house here in St. Thomas and began divorce proceedings. It's been a year—but I'm still not in the forgiving mood—not even a little bit. He blew it big time."

He runs his fingers through his hair.

"Hey—how about we go explore that little island over there. I bet the view from the top is really spectacular."

Marisa stands and slowly follows Alexis down the rocky beach as a brisk wind whips through the sun-drenched sand.

8
Frenchman's Reef Resort

"Uh-huh—that's right—send only your best wine. Two in fact—add it to my bill—include a lobster in the deal also."

Victoria de Hoya nods several times and shuts off her cell phone as she faces the panoramic view of the harbor. She sighs loudly as she walks toward the open balcony and smiles.

"It'll be so good to see Sandra and Scott again. Who knew she would turn what happened two years ago into a book."

She licks her lips and grins.

"I guess I shouldn't really be surprised after she managed to snag that good-looking rascal all for herself. I bet their sex life is endless nights of passionate lovemaking—lucky her."

She pulls a strand of hair out of her face.

"I wonder if Sandra knows any hot eligible bachelors."

She sighs loudly and faces the hotel room.

"Eligible straight bachelors—must like women."

She walks over to the mini bar and pauses briefly.

"When did my life become so boring?"

Victoria reaches for a glass just as her cell phone begins to ring. She glances at it and shrugs. On the screen she sees a photo of Milo. Several images appear seconds later. She sighs.

9
Australia

A man nervously looks back several times as he runs toward a terminal and smirks. Silas Bell seems in a rush as he heads toward a nearby ticket booth. He shrugs as he gives a ticket to an attendant and smiles as he's waved through.

"Uh-huh—they thought they had me—but not quite. I'm so out of here. Got to look for greener pastures if I want to stay ahead of the game—starting with my little bro—bet he never thought he'd see me again. Especially after what happened all those years ago—I'm sure he's forgotten what I did to him and his mother—it's not like I was to blame—that spider could've ended up anywhere—even between the blankets as they slept."

He smiles and walks toward a row of seats inside an airplane as other people begin making their way past him.

10
Blakely Mansion

Astrid Blakely sighs loudly as she watches her son dive into the pool headfirst. As the water splashes all over the surface of the tiled walkway Byron Blakely jumps out of the water with a huge grin on his face. He sees her reaction and sighs loudly.

"Did you see? Did you see what I did?"

Astrid seems upset.

"I saw. Who taught you to do something so dangerous? You could've cracked your head—or worse broken you neck."

Byron rolls his eyes and sighs loudly.

"Niels showed me. His trainer taught him."

Page **26**

Astrid throws a towel to her eight-year-old-son and seems annoyed as he glances at the pool again. He grins broadly.

"I want to do it again."

Astrid raises her hand in the air.

"No way—once is enough for today."

Byron seems upset as he begins drying his body.

"You're no fun—you never let me do anything. Niels gets to do whatever he wants. He never hears no—never—ever."

Astrid points her finger at Byron.

"I'll remember that when they're lowering his coffin into a grave after he gets killed jumping off some cliff or other."

Byron seems confused and turns away.

11
Mountain Top

"Of course I didn't tell her everything."

Brent sighs loudly as he glances at the road ahead. As he passes several large trees he glances at the cell phone in his hands and glares at Derek Ving on the screen. He shrugs.

"My sister is in a need-to-know basis. It's best that way—if she knew what I have planned she might switch sides on me."

Derek rolls his eyes knowingly.

"Uh-huh—I know her deal—she caught me having a private moment with her friend from high school and flipped."

He laughs slyly and points at Brent.

"What's a guy to do when presented with an opportunity to have an intense blowjob in a supermarket parking lot?"

Brent seems annoyed and sighs loudly.

"Spare me the details with what happened at Pueblo last month. Don't really want to know about you getting a blowjob from some nasty whore my sister thought was her best friend."

Derek laughs loudly and gestures.

"My dick hasn't been the same since."

Brent pulls over to the side of the road and grimaces. He watches Derek making a lewd gesture with his finger.

"If I were you I'd be careful where my sister is concerned and your dick—she might just chop it off—made threats."

Derek makes a lewd gesture with his finger again as he seems to revel in Brent's reaction. Brent waves his hand.

"Enough with your sexual escapades—we have a lot of work to do in order to make sure that brat doesn't push us to the frigging edge. Astrid Blakely is sitting on a wad of cash. Take her son and that cash is as good as mine. Kid won't know squat."

Derek shoots Brent a knowing look.

"I expect my cut as promised. Stashing that brat will be quite a chore. Babysitting some spoiled rich kid isn't going to be a picnic—he'll probably be terribly mouthy—think he's all that."

Brent shakes his fist at Derek.

"He'll play along or else we'll tie him up."

He laughs slyly.

"Put the fear of God into him."

Derek grins broadly and nods several times.

12
New York City

"Don't you get cute on me—we had a deal."

Roland Parker leans back in his chair and sighs loudly.

"Uh-huh—you're gonna do it—no compromises. I'll expect you to give me a print-ready copy by the end of the week."

He laughs loudly.

"That's right Malone—I intend to be a dick about the whole deal—make you see the light if necessary. You owe me plenty after taking two months off—two very long months."

He stands and walks toward the window.

"Tell Sandra I said hi."

He nods a few times and shuts off his cell phone. He turns to face the office and grins. He gestures with his hands.

"That man can be so annoying. Thinks the whole world revolves around him. Ugh—makes me so sick sometimes."

He grins broadly as he looks at the city.

"Look at the view—it's almost like a postcard."

Scott Malone turns to look at Sandra King with a huge grin spread out across his face. He runs his fingers through his hair and watches Sandra's reaction. She slowly walks over toward him.

"What are you going to do about Roland?"

Scott gestures with his hand.

"I'm thinking of taking a hit out on him."

He laughs loudly.

"Some cement shoes would do nicely right before he takes a header off the Brooklyn Bridge. He might even scream as he falls into the water knowing I was laughing gleefully."

Sandra pinches Scott.

"I'm serious—what are you gonna do about him calling every hour. That man is seriously stroking my last nerve."

Scott pulls Sandra toward him.

"He wants a story on our upcoming visit to Mysterious Island. Thinks it'll grab plenty interest from readers of your book—Parker thinks the story has fallen out of the headlines recently if truth be known—he's intent on milking the drama for everything nevertheless—seems quite restless actually."

Sandra seems upset and shrugs.

"Is he still upset that Maureen left him?"

Scott nods several times.

"Uh-huh—mopes around his office all the time from what I hear—wishes he'd done things much differently—blames being a workaholic on his marriage ending—at least that's the impression I got when I talked to him earlier—tough break—rough."

Sandra runs her fingers through Scott's hair. They look at each other for a few seconds. She gives him a knowing look.

"I'm glad you're here with me—don't like being away from you—like your company—like how we get along so well."

Scott laughs loudly and kisses Sandra.

"Such nice words from my wife—a guy can get spoiled really badly—expect it all the time. Hugs and kisses too."

Sandra lets her fingers stroke Scott's cheek.

"I don't regret one minute of marrying you—we have a past—plenty of drama to remember—especially after."

Scott grins and faces the balcony.

"Think I should fix Roland up with someone?"

Sandra wags her finger at Scott.

"Don't even think of it—good intentions always end badly. Let him find his way—deal with his divorce from Maureen."

She jabs him in the chest.

"I mean it Scott—don't you even think about fixing him up with someone—he'll be pissed—angry actually—angry enough to send you to India on a story out of spite—maybe St. Helena."

Scott looks at Sandra slyly and laughs.

"I hear St. Helena is beautiful this time of year."

Sandra playfully jabs Scott again.

"I mean it—leave it be."

He reaches for his cell phone and grins.

14

Alexis and Marisa get into his jeep. Seconds later he starts the engine and glances at her. He grins broadly and sighs.

"We've got to do this again."

Marisa playfully slides her fingers across his belt buckle and laughs. Alexis grins broadly as he watches her. He winks.

"Nothing beats having an intense sexual experience on a deserted beach. Quite a nice moment no doubt—relaxing."

Marisa tugs at the belt buckle again.

"I'm glad you were my first."

Alexis grins and leans over to kiss Marisa.

"I've never felt this way about anyone before."

Marisa wipes a tear from her eye.

"What about your parents?"

Alexis seems upset and turns away.

Page **30**

"What about them?"

Marisa reaches out to gently touch his hand.

"Your folks think we're too young."

Alexis waves his hand in the air and shrugs.

"They can't tell me what to do—not after the mess they made of their own lives—trust me, my folks have more problems than the characters in that old TV series from the 1980s called *Flamingo Road*. All they did was fight before they split for good. I was always caught in the middle—hoping things would get better. Then my father began banging Celia—and things got even worse—especially after I caught them having sex together."

He runs his fingers through his hair.

15

"I swear this place is like a maze—couldn't find the right suite—it took me ten whole minutes to figure things out."

Justin turns to look toward the harbor in a distance as he takes another swig from the drink in his hand. He laughs.

"But enough of me—I just spoke with the owner of the bookstore before I got here and she told me there are already two thousand orders for your book. Several hundred of those are slated to show up for the signing. She's pretty excited."

Sandra turns to look at Scott.

"I guess that means we can take that vacation to the Maldives next year—get far away from Roland Parker."

Scott laughs and points at Sandra.

"Uh-huh—don't count on it. He'll find us."

Justin takes another swig of his drink and grins. He notices a copy of Sandra's book on a table nearby. He gestures.

"Things are looking up already."

He runs his fingers through his hair.

"Your book has the potential to smash records from what I've heard from several people I know. They think it could set a record in Europe too—London especially. You might even get a royal invite if we play our cards right—meet the royal family."

Sandra rolls her eyes and glances at Scott briefly. Justin notices and quickly turns away. He wipes sweat from his brow.

"I've booked you for the next six weeks all over the country. By the time we're done your book will clear one million. No **Margaret Mitchell** numbers or **Anne Frank** for that matter but still quite good considering just a month ago hardly anyone knew your name and now it looks like your book will become one of the year's biggest selling books. A movie is certainly going to happen now—big stars and glitzy premieres in Los Angeles, New York and London—detailed interviews on the red carpet."

Justin walks toward the balcony and stops suddenly.

"Have you ever written a screenplay?"

Sandra seems confused.

The Next Day

16
Main Street

"I'll see you in an hour—probably earlier."

Astrid nods several times and shuts off her cell phone as she faces her friend. Norma Crowe shoots Astrid a warning look as she notices someone in a distance. Astrid turns to look in the direction of where Norma is looking. She seems upset.

"I thought you said he left the island?"

Astrid grits her teeth.

"I thought he did—haven't seen him in years."

Several yards away Brent is sitting at a cafe chatting with a woman Astrid doesn't recognize. She shakes her head.

"He's probably trying his latest moves on her. Still playing the same game he always played with me—but pretending he isn't actually a loser. Ugh—I ought to walk over there and tell her how much trouble he'll be once he beds her. Damn him."

Norma grabs Astrid's arm.

"Don't you dare do such a thing—he'll come after you again—beat you up like he did before—and cheat on you."

Astrid seems upset and grimaces.

"Ugh—he makes me so angry—only wanted to get his hands on my money—pretended he cared—used me."

Norma leads Astrid down the street.

"Uh-huh—his type never changes. Let's just forget you ever saw him today—think of Peter—think of how much he loves you—think of your upcoming wedding in a few months."

Astrid smiles broadly.

"Peter Zimmerman definitely is a keeper. No toad is he. I got lucky when I wasn't even looking. He's a good man."

Norma nods in agreement.

"How about we make our way to Havensight and have a drink at that new health food bar that opened last month?"

Astrid nods and lets Norma lead her away.

17
Drake's Seat

"I don't get him—why can't he just leave me alone? Let me live my own life—it's not fair. He doesn't understand."

Alexis wipes sweat from his brow.

"He treats me like I'm his personal property."

Marisa reaches out to touch Alexis's hand as he shuts off his cell phone and looks at her. She nods in agreement.

"When did your father say he was gonna drop by?"

Alexis rolls his eyes.

"He didn't actually say. Said something about mending fences with my mother—make things right. Ugh—there's nothing to fix after what he did to her—she had every right to dump his sorry ass after he played doctor with that sleazy whore."

He angrily clenches his fist and sighs.

"She wasn't the first one either—he probably dipped his wick plenty of times into every stupid whore that gave him the time of day. I bet I have plenty of brothers and sisters out there that I don't know about—won't find out until the will reading."

Marisa reacts and pulls away from Alexis.

"Do you think you have siblings you don't know about? Would your father keep something like that from you?"

Alexis wipes sweat from his brow again and nods.

"Uh-huh he would—no doubt about it."

Alexis grimaces.

"I'm a poor little rich boy."

Marisa gives Alexis an odd look.

"What do you mean by that?"

Alexis glances at his cell phone.

"I have everything—everything but parents that love me."

Marisa seems upset as she touches Alexis's hand.

"Don't your parents love you?"

Alexis faces Marisa and sighs loudly.

"There's no love in my family—none that matters anyway as far as I'm concerned. Money doesn't buy happiness."

Alexis opens the car door and slowly steps out. He faces the panoramic view of Magens Bay Beach far below. He sighs.

"Sometimes I wish I didn't have a penny to my name in return for a family that was normal. Wish I had parents that loved each other and not how much frigging money they had. Ugh—my life sucks chunks. Now I know how **Barbara Hutton** felt."

Marisa steps out of the car and looks around.

"Was she a movie star or something?"

Alexis waves his hand in the air.

"She was an heir to the massive Woolworth fortune. Her grandfather **F. W. Woolworth** founded a chain of department stores back in the day. She had everything she could ever want in life—everything but love. Her life was anything but happy."

Marisa reaches out to hug Alexis.

"I didn't know."

Alexis sighs loudly.

"Maybe my cousin had the right idea."

Alexis slowly turns around to face the street.

"She lives in Los Angeles. Turned her back on the family fortune in order to live her own life—she's an actress now."

He runs his hands through his hair and shrugs.

Page **34**

"Last time I talked to Laura she said she was happy that she made the move—especially after *what* happened."

Marisa reacts and seems confused.

"What do you mean by that?"

Alexis turns to face the ocean again.

"Laura was one of the people that ended up on that island that has become a tourist attraction. Said it was the scariest thing she's ever faced. Worst than her parents fighting all the time over money—worst than catching her stepfather fucking a dude at her mother's condo in San Juan. Incident freaked her out so much she won't be coming back for a book signing by one of the people who lived through it—scared of coming back actually."

Marisa reaches out to Alexis again.

18
Fort Christian

"I don't believe in ghosts. Never have and never will. I'd have to see it to be a believer. See it in person myself."

June McQueen rolls her eyes at Wendy Crowe as they stand in front of the imposing structure several yards away.

"I heard it was built in the 1670s when the first settlers arrived—and all sorts of horrible things happened throughout the years. People died—and some came back. Haunting some of the rooms where they died. Gruesome endings were plenty."

Wendy begins laughing.

"Uh-huh—I see you've been watching too much freaky programs on the Discovery Channel. But I remain skeptical of old junk like that—ghosts aren't real—just stories by people who have too much time on their hands or are seriously unstable."

June gestures at Fort Christian.

"I dare you to go inside."

Wendy gives June an odd look and turns away.

"I've got better things to do."

June watches as Wendy pulls out her cell phone. She gives her a knowing look which Wendy notices. She points at June.

"Besides—I'm waiting for a call from Cliff."

June sticks her finger in her mouth.

"Ugh—I thought you were finally over him—especially after he sampled Donna Manjack last week at Tyler's party."

Wendy seems upset and waves her hand.

"He said she came on to him—seduced him."

June grabs Wendy's arm.

"Uh-huh—but it wasn't her hand inside his underwear that you saw—it was his finger inside her vagina—face it he's a dog who played you for a fool—time you got real with that creep."

Wendy glances at the cell phone in her hand.

"Cliff Nickerson is my first love—I can't help how I feel. He said I was his first. Said we had a connection—lasting love."

June stifles a laughs and shakes her head.

"I'll just bet he feeds that corny line to all the girls he's bedded and discarded. Cliff Nickerson was not a virgin when he met you—not even a little—been around—soiled his share of girls all over St. Thomas—and St. John too from what I heard."

Wendy seems irritated by the statement.

"I don't care one way or the other—I feel the way I do and nothing will change that. Cliff and I are destined to be together for the rest of our lives—I want him to father my children."

June throws her hands up in the air.

19
Windward Passage Hotel

Silas throws a suitcase carelessly onto the bed as he glances at the view of Hassel Island across from the hotel.

"Uh-huh—I'm going to like it here. Plenty of sunshine and luscious babes—oh yeah—this is going to be a sweet vacation."

He grins broadly and licks his lips.

"Time to make contact with my little bro as I plot out my revenge—get what's rightfully mine—pretend I care."

He laughs as he walks over to a mini bar not far away from the sliding glass doors that front a balcony of the tiny room.

"Once I'm done with Armand I'll never have to worry about money again. Live life on my terms—which is only fair."

He waves his hand in the air several times.

"With him out of the way, his share of the inheritance will be mine. Then I go after Houghton Fawcett for what he did to my father—pay him back royally—make him suffer terribly."

He begins laughing hysterically.

"Afterwards I'll return to Australia and make sure Serena Glick pays dearly for locking me up in that nuthouse. She'll suffer most of all no doubt—starting with watching her son die."

He pours himself a drink and laughs again.

20

"I'm here for you if you need me."

Alexis turns around to face Marisa. They kiss.

"I appreciate that—appreciate it more than you know."

Marisa hugs Alexis tightly.

"How about we go get a burger?"

Alexis nods.

21
Magens Bay Beach

Sandra shuffles her feet in the sand as Scott stares out at sea. She stops and faces him. He purposely ignores her.

"What's going on in that mind of yours?"

Scott grins slyly.

"Wouldn't you like to know?"

Sandra jabs him several times.

"I have a right to know—I demand it."

Scott laughs again.

"I'll think about it."

Sandra jabs him again as he smiles broadly.

"What are you up to Scott?"

He pulls her toward him and smirks.

"I was just thinking how famous you might get—might get bored with me—expect more from me—lots of drama."

Sandra reaches out to stroke Scott's cheek.

"I want nothing more than we have already. I'm not gonna trade you in for someone else—you're stuck with me."

Scott grins broadly.

"In that case—I think we need to talk."

Sandra looks at Scott nervously.

"What's going on? Did you do something stupid?"

Scott shakes his head.

"Not yet—but I'm thinking about it."

Sandra playfully jabs Scott again as he faces the beach.

"What did Roland Parker ask you to do now?"

Scott pulls out his cell phone.

"See for yourself."

Sandra gasps in shock.

22
Frenchman's Reef Resort

"Uh-huh—I was on that island two years ago. Saw those guys up close—had nightmares for weeks afterwards. It wasn't like the movies where everyone gets saved at the last minute."

Victoria watches the reaction on the waiter's face.

"I thought we were done for—their guns were drawn."

She sighs loudly and seems upset.

"Then it happened—we saw these military types dropping in from the sky—while bullets were flying everywhere."

Casey Tyverton seems in awe as he sighs.

"Well, I'm glad you're OK."

He turns to leave and stops suddenly.

"Are you going to be at the book sighing?"

Victoria nods.

"Uh-huh—I'll be there."

Casey wipes sweat from his brow and grins.

"Then I'll see you at the bookshop."

Victoria watches as he pushes the trays of food out the door. As the door closes she leans against the wall and sighs.

"Maybe I should write a book too—as therapy."

She seems bothered and shrugs.

<h3 style="text-align:center">23</h3>

"I already told you I don't believe in ghosts—there are no such things out there—the dead can't walk again for any reason whatsoever—dead is dead—once you kick it you're done."

June points to her cell phone.

"You don't know that for sure Wendy—just because you can't see something doesn't mean there's nothing there—there are just things that can't be explained. This is the Caribbean after all—all sorts of weird things have happened here that can't be explained by ignoring it. I've talked to people about stories I've heard—heard of things that could possibly be—zombies for example—it's not like on TV—but possible nevertheless."

Wendy opens to the door to her car.

"Just because people believe what they've been told by a bunch of kooks doesn't change anything—nothing beats seeing it for yourself without the help of another person influencing you to believe in something they may or may not have seen with their own two eyes. I know about how legends start—and this island is flooded with them—but it still doesn't change anything."

June gets into the car and shuts the door.

"I know what my great-grandmother told me."

Wendy gives June a knowing look.

"I've heard the story already—and I explained to you that your great-grandmother didn't hear a werewolf knocking on the door outside her house late at night back in the 1940s—and she didn't hear it howl in the nearby woods either. It just isn't possible—werewolves don't exist—no different than UFOs."

June shakes her finger at Wendy.

"My great-grandmother didn't tell lies."

Wendy grabs June's arm.

Page 39

"I never said she did—all I said was it couldn't have happened the way she described it—there's an explanation that makes more sense than a werewolf story. What she heard that night was a branch banging against the side of the house."

Wendy lets go of June's arm.

"You told me that her house was located in the middle of the woods—with trees growing everywhere—close to the house. Heavy winds could make the branches from the nearby trees bang against the house—making it appear something was knocking on the door when in actuality it was a tree branch."

June rolls her eyes and sighs.

"How do you explain the howling?"

Wendy seems annoyed and shrugs.

"It was a dog—probably lost and calling out for help."

June runs her fingers through her hair.

"Fine—whatever—but that doesn't explain ghostly events that have happened to people—and it just wasn't one either."

Wendy leans against the steering wheel.

"I already told you that everything can be explained."

June grabs her cell phone and begins hastily searching the Internet as Wendy waits patiently. Suddenly June stops.

"Explain the **Chase Vaults of Barbados**."

Wendy seems confused.

"What are you talking about?"

June waves her hand in front of Wendy's face.

"No one has ever been able to explain what happened on that island back in 1812. What happened in that little cemetery in Barbados remains unsolved to this day—no answers."

Wendy glances at June's cell phone.

"Everyone lies on the Internet."

June rolls her eyes and points at her cell phone.

"Except that the story of what took place in 1812 involving the death of **Dorcas Chase** was mentioned in books written at the time—the Internet didn't make this story up. It really happened two hundred years ago—and since that time no one has ever been able to find any proof it was a hoax—no one."

"That doesn't mean anything at all—doesn't prove it really happened—one way or the other—it's just an urban legend."

June angrily shuts off her cell phone.

"Uh-huh—I see you have nothing to say when you can't prove your theory that everything can be explained. Just face it Wendy, there are things that can't be explained—no matter how much skeptics might want to dismiss certain things as a figment of someone's imagination—proving it false isn't so easy."

Wendy points her finger at June.

"This is why you can't get laid—what guy would want to deal with your fascination into all things weird? No one that's who—not even Hadley Black would thread down that road. He's a nerd no doubt—but even he prefers to steer clear of you and all the crap you talk about concerning island lore—take a hint."

June rolls her eyes again and shrugs.

"Hadley and I are just friends—nothing more—he spends too much time reading and not enough time thinking about girls—his mother keeps a tight leash on him—watches him."

Wendy reacts and sighs loudly.

"Ugh—don't go there with Hadley and his mother. I've heard she makes him keep his bedroom door open at night."

June shoots Wendy a look of disgust.

24
Havensight Mall

"Uh-huh—keep your eye on her. Make sure you know her routine before we grab the brat—I don't want any mistakes."

Brent grins slyly as he faces the parking lot.

TO BE CONTINUED

A Brief Look at the Second Episode

Poor relationship choices are hastily made by several individuals as a long-lost brother arrives for an extended visit while a jilted ex-boyfriend moves ahead with his diabolical blackmail plan.

Episode 2
Blood and Roses

1
Blakely Mansion

"Things are a mess right now. We might have to delay our trip for about a week—maybe two. I've got to play nice with a few suits coming for a visit next week—stuffed shirts types."

Astrid Blakely gives Peter Zimmerman a curious look as she tousles his hair. She slides her finger across his cheek.

"You're threading on thin ice—dangerously so."

He laughs as he leans back in his chair.

"It's out of my hands—I'm just a ragdoll until they get back on a plane for the mainland. These things happen—deal."

Astrid kisses Peter and begins unzipping his pants.

"Seems to me you'd better make it up to me in other ways—a girlfriend can get really annoyed if her boyfriend spends too much time ignoring her—might want to get even."

Peter grins broadly and sighs.

"Where's Byron?"

Astrid waves her hand in the air.

"What's it to you?"

Peter gives Astrid a knowing look.

"A man needs to know certain things before he can make a decision concerning his girlfriend—intimate decisions."

"He's with my mother at Coral World."

Peter watches Astrid's fingers pull at the zipper of his pants and he begins laughing. They jump up and run toward the bedroom down the hall in less than ten seconds. The door slams shut followed by sounds of clothes coming off in a rush.

2

Market Square

"Ugh—look at her playing her game. Look at how she's making a fool out of him. Yuk—I think I'm gonna be sick."

Marisa Rossmore makes a gagging gesture with her finger as she looks at Alexis de Hoya sitting across from her.

"Ugh—she's such a disgusting slut—goes from one guy to another—spreads her legs just to get what she wants—lies to every guy she meets—pretends she really cares about them."

Alexis reaches out to touch Marisa's hand as he looks at where Ava Fontaine and Greg Forbes are sitting. He shrugs.

"Let it go—Greg can handle his own—he knows what's going on—just wants to get a piece—he's not innocent."

Marisa faces Alexis and sighs loudly.

"I know all about Greg Forbes—he's made a career of hopping from bed to bed—but *her*—ugh—she's so skanky."

Alexis takes a bite of his ketchup-drenched hamburger and snaps his fingers in front of Marisa's face several times.

"I know what she did to your brother—pretended she was carrying his child—made a fool of him for a month—then the truth came out and she got caught—exposed by her private tutor of all people—admitted he was the daddy—got busted for fooling around with a high school girl—awaiting trial as we speak."

Marisa continues glaring at Ava.

"She lost the baby soon after—claimed she fell down the stairs—said she slipped—but I heard she did it on purpose."

Page **44**

Alexis reacts and stops eating. He sighs.

"I wouldn't put stock in anything Dana Waymore says. She has a rep for embellishing what she hears to her advantage."

Marisa waves her hand in the air and shrugs.

"Dana Waymore was Ava's best friend—so she would know what really happened—she said it wasn't an accident."

She lowers her voice and leans closer to Alexis. Her face wreaths into a smile as she taps her finger on top of the table.

"Dana said after her tutor admitted he'd been sleeping with Ava, she threw herself down the stairs hoping Simon would come back to her. But he didn't—not after I told him what Dana told me. I'm just glad he's finally rid of her—*ugh*—I hate her."

Alexis leans back in his chair.

"How's Simon doing?"

Marisa stifles a wicked smile.

"He's in Miami—attending college. He has a new girlfriend too—says she's nothing like Ava—doesn't lie endlessly."

Alexis notices Ava standing up and watches as she stares at Marisa. Seconds later she grabs Greg's arm and begins walking toward where he and Marisa are sitting. People stop and look.

"*Oh*—if it isn't Marisa Rossmore trying to dig her claws into a bag of money—so very sad—but then again—tacky."

Marisa flies into a rage and slaps Ava.

"I see you've moved on from your tutor to Greg. But wait—did you bother to tell Greg his brother fucked you at Lauren's party? Bryce said you were so drunk—bragged about taking you in Lauren's pool house—said you were easy."

Ava turns to look at Greg and then at Marisa.

"You *bitch*—that never happened. I barely know Bryce. He and I spoke once at Lauren's party. His girlfriend was there."

Marisa licks her lips and laughs slyly.

"Bryce said there are pictures of him sticking you that night—courtesy of Omar Cortez. Ask anyone—a picture is worth a thousand words—millions in fact. How about I call Omar?"

Ava seems in shock as she bolts from the diner while Greg continues to stand there with a confused look on his face.

Page **45**

<h1 style="text-align:center">3
Washington DC</h1>

"Uh-huh—I got your message loud and clear—wouldn't miss it for a second—can't wait to see you and that chump you married—tell him I said that by the way—piss him off a bit."

Maxwell Pendergraft grins broadly.

"No doubt—but I can take him any day he wants—tell him that too—let him know I boxed in college—quite dangerous."

He laughs and walks toward the pieces of luggage at the front door of his apartment. He gestures with his hand.

"No problem—you know I'd do anything to help sell your book—what happened to you guys is an instant page-turner."

He smiles as he reaches for the doorknob.

<h1 style="text-align:center">4
Mafolie Hotel</h1>

"I'll see you tomorrow morning—booked you a hotel room where we're staying—it's got a nice view of the harbor."

Sandra King nods several times and turns to face Scott Malone as she shuts off her cell phone. He seems upset.

"Was that loser Maxwell Pendergraft talking trash about me again? You'd think he'd know better after I whipped his ass at tennis—said he was really good at the game. He wasn't."

Sandra walks over to where Scott is sitting.

"You and Maxwell can have a rematch when he arrives tomorrow—might be interesting to see which one of you is better at telling tall tales. He's quite the charmer too—hooked up with Victoria less than an hour after they met—she smiled for a week afterwards—said he knew how to treat a woman in bed."

Scott rolls his eyes knowingly.

"Uh-huh—I'll just bet he knows how to please a woman in bed—dude is so righteous—never plays games—boring."

Sandra tousles Scott's hair and grins.

Page 46

"Is that a streak of jealousy I hear?"

Scott waves his hand in the air and laughs.

"I've got nothing to be jealous about when it comes to the likes of Maxwell Pendergraft. I'm way better looking."

Sandra leans over to kiss him on the lips.

"That's what he said you'd say."

Scott grins broadly and kisses Sandra again.

5

Marisa watches as Ava storms out of the diner. Greg stands motionless for a few seconds and then follows her.

"Would love to be a fly on the wall when Omar shows Greg those photos of his brother on top of Ava—plowing her over and over—knowing his good buddy was standing nearby."

Alexis reacts and looks at the door.

"You were quite nasty to her—over the top."

Marisa shrugs and gestures wildly with her hand.

"She hurt my brother—made a fool of him—screwed with his feelings. Payback is a bitch—I've been waiting a while for the right moment—bet you anything she'll try to lie her way out of this mess—blame everyone but herself—play the victim."

They watch as a few people leave the diner and venture out into the empty sidewalk nearby. He sighs loudly.

"You'd better watch your back. Ava's gonna be out for blood—your blood—she'll strike when you least expect."

Marisa looks at the sidewalk again.

"I'm not worried. She's always been a bitch—and everyone knows it. She has no friends—none that are real anyway."

She stifles a laugh and seems pleased.

"She burned her bridges with Dana by telling everyone Dana slept with her tennis coach—which was a lie—he's gay. There's absolutely no coming back after what she did. Ava is all alone and she's got no one to thank but her own behavior."

Marisa stands up and looks around.

"Are you gonna be OK with facing your dad?"

Alexis faces Marisa as she glances at the front door.

"I'm good—he knows he messed up royally. It's up to him to try and mend fences. If he refuses—nothing will change."

He watches as Marisa takes his hand.

6

"I'm assuming that gigantic smile on your face is telling me you really enjoyed what just happened between us?"

Peter nods as he pulls Astrid toward him and kisses her before he gets into his car. He gives her a knowing look.

"I'm quite relaxed."

Astrid smirks as he starts the engine.

"I'll be back in an hour or so. Got a few things to clear up with several of the new recruits—shouldn't take too long."

Astrid blows him a kiss as he drives away. As he drives away she notices a car coming up the driveway. She sighs.

"I guess that's the new nanny."

She watches as the car pulls to a stop.

7
Royal Dane Mall

"I hate her. I hate that selfish bitch. She's always trying to insult me. What I wouldn't give to seriously pay her back."

Ava gestures with her hand as she and Greg walk along a narrow passageway while they pass several handicraft stores.

"I'd be willing to help."

Ava turns around to face Greg and smiles.

"What do you have in mind?"

Greg stops.

"Make it look like she's two-timing that rich geek. Make him think he's being played—bust them up. Fuck her over."

Ava licks her lips several times.

"I like how you think Greg—but how would we go about something like that? They're always together—like twins."

Greg leans against the wall nearby.

"Lane Rolfe owes me a favor."

He makes a lewd gesture with his finger.

"I covered for him when he played doctor with that chick from Virgin Gorda last year. Jennifer Isberg never had a clue."

Ava seems confused and shrugs.

"Didn't she ditch him for her sister's boyfriend?"

Greg nods several times and laughs.

"Uh-huh—but she never found out he played around before she got bored with him—courtesy of yours truly."

He laughs and pulls out his cell phone.

"He owes me."

Ava pulls Greg toward her.

"I like how devious your mind works."

Greg grins broadly.

"That's not the only thing that works really well."

Ava's eyes follows Greg's glance. She notices his erection swelling under his tight Lycra shorts. He smirks slyly.

8

"I'm looking forward to meeting Byron."

Savannah Windsor turns around to face Astrid as the scenic view of the Charlotte Amalie looms in the background.

"Does he like sports?"

Astrid nods and points to a baseball bat lying several yards away against some potted plants. Savannah grins.

9

Havensight Mall

"Uh-huh—that's right—my sister is with Astrid right now. That stupid bitch has no idea what's about to happen. My sister is playing her part well—it won't be long before we start playing our game using Astrid's brat as insurance—money in the bank."

Brent Crawford laughs as he turns around.

Page **49**

"Savannah will take him to Magens on Friday. Then we drop in on them and grab the brat—tie him up—cover his fucking mouth with duct tape—and then call that wretched bitch."

He looks at his cell phone and grins broadly.

10
Water Island

"Uh-huh—got it—I'm game—us guys gotta stick together when it comes to someone like Marisa Rossmore. She and I have history as you know—refused to go down on me last year."

Lane Rolfe seems upset and sighs.

"I asked for a frigging blowjob and she turned me down. Said I was dirt—fooled around too much with skanks."

He laughs again as he notices Whitney Wilkins looking at him while her head bobs up and down on his erect penis.

"I'll call you later—hammer out the details—right now I got urgent things to attend to—about to blow a massive load."

He laughs slyly as he shuts off his cell phone. He smirks.

"When did you say your parents were due back?"

Whitney looks up at him again and shrugs.

11
Frenchtown

"This will do nicely for what I have planned. Thanks for going through that extra mile—I really appreciate it."

Ingrid de Hoya watches the reaction from the waiter as he shuts the door to her car. He nods and walks away as she turns to face the parking lot. She runs her fingers through her hair.

"Do you think I'm pushing things?"

She faces Allegra Penn with a worried look on her face.

"It's time you began dating again—and Jordan McKinney is as nice as they come—excellent photographer too."

Ingrid leans against the car.

"I just don't want to screw up again."

Allegra shakes her head and sighs.

"How long have you and I been best friends?"

Ingrid gives Allegra a knowing look and grimaces.

"Is this where you give me a lecture?"

Allegra walks over to Ingrid.

"It's time to move on—it's over with Alexander. He made his choice—and it wasn't you that he chose. Game over."

Ingrid nods in agreement and shrugs.

12

Back Street Cafe

"It's what it is—I'm not a virgin—never claimed to be pure and righteous—fooled around plenty in the last four years."

Bryce Forbes makes a lewd gesture with his finger as he looks at Isabel Black noticing her shocked stare. He smirks.

"If you want a nice guy to pop you then I suggest you keep looking—I've been around—fucked plenty—not sorry I did."

He laughs as she reacts.

"I've got a rep—girls know my deal."

He reaches over to touch her hand and grins.

"You'll never be the same again."

He makes a lewd gesture with his tongue.

"Every guy will want a piece of you if you let me do the honors. No one will say no to you again—I guarantee it."

He pulls her hand toward him.

"My dick has power."

He watches as her eyes wander toward his belt buckle. He grins broadly as he watches his swelling erection. Isabel sighs.

"What if I get pregnant?"

Bryce waves his hand in the air and notices Wendy Crowe coming toward him. He grins broadly as they embrace.

"Haven't seen you in a while?"

Wendy glances at Isabel and then at Bryce.

"I've been busy—had plenty on my plate earlier."

Bryce gives her a knowing look.

Page 51

"I heard you and Cliff might be on the skids—I'm here if you need me—could pencil you in tonight if need be."

Wendy pretends to slap Bryce.

"You and I are never gonna happen—not even if Cliff and I split. You've simply soiled too many girls—terrible rep."

Bryce pretends to be hurt by the comment.

"You always seem to know how to wound a guy in the worse way—crush his ego—make him feel like a total loser."

Wendy wags her finger at Bryce.

"You said it—I didn't."

She turns to look at Isabel and sighs.

"Shouldn't you be hanging out with your dorky cousin?"

Isabel glances at Bryce and then glares at Wendy.

"Shouldn't you be wondering where Cliff Nickerson is at the moment? If I were you I'd be worried he wasn't on top of some girl he met at Antilles School—people say—you know."

Wendy shoots Isabel a harsh look and walks away without saying another word. Bryce grins as Isabel faces him again.

"Oh man, that was vicious."

Isabel shrugs and watches as Wendy leaves the cafe.

"She had it coming—always thinks she knows everything about everyone—not so much if you want the truth—especially where Cliff is concerned—heard he was scouting new prospects earlier today—cruising around Antilles School according to my friend who goes there—said he made his play with a couple of her friends—asked for their numbers—played it really casual."

Bryce winks at Isabel and laughs.

"No doubt Cliff Nickerson will be calling you after you give it up to me—obviously he's not taking Wendy too seriously."

Isabel seems pleased and nods.

13
Magens Bay Beach

"I thought we already decided to keep things between us on a friendly basis—it's the best I can do—concerning Trevor."

Page **52**

Armand Bell watches as Jasmine Rossmore turns away as she watches their son making a sand castle several feet away with a few other children. Armand reaches out to Jasmine.

"I'm sorry—but I thought I made it clear when I came back from the island—I'm just not into you. I moved on. I'm sorry."

Jasmine pulls away from Armand.

"I wasn't expecting us to get back together Armand. But I was hoping you'd see me as something other than your son's mother. I thought we were friends—especially after."

Armand runs his fingers through his hair.

"It's just awkward—what else do you want me to say?"

He glances again at Trevor Bell playing nearby.

"It was a shock when you told me. But I adjusted even before my mother read me the riot act. She let me have it for weeks afterwards—demanded I marry you—settle down."

Jasmine seems upset.

"I'm sorry."

Armand shakes his head.

"Don't worry about it. She and I have an understanding concerning my private life now—and about my girlfriends."

Jasmine turns to look at Trevor again.

14
Miami

"Maxwell? Maxwell Pendergraft is that really you?"

As he turns around to respond a huge grin spreads across Maxwell's face as he sees Diana Munroe looking at him.

"I can't believe it—we're on the same flight."

Diana reaches out to embrace Maxwell. They hug for a few seconds. He watches as she sits down beside him.

"I guess you're going to the book signing also?"

Diana nods and leans toward.

"Sandra's publicist thought it would be great if everyone who was mentioned in her book showed up for a photo shoot at the bookstore signing—everyone that survived anyway."

Page **53**

She notices Maxwell's reaction and shrugs. He watches as she glances at the zipper on his jeans. He waves his hand.

"I'm still single—love being a bachelor."

Diana grins broadly.

"I'm staying at a hotel downtown—Windward Passage."

She leans closer to him and whispers.

"I wouldn't mind it at all if you insisted on a threesome again—likes a guy that enjoys women—likes fucking."

Maxwell waves his hand in the air.

"I think we can certainly work something out no doubt while I'm in the islands—enjoyed our last encounter."

He watches as her fingers slowly glide over his leg.

"Is Laura Wiley joining you?"

Diana shakes her head and sighs.

"No—she's still freaked out about what happened—said she couldn't handle it—really likes living in Los Angeles."

Maxwell nods as his cell phone rings. He shuts it off and faces Diana again. She looks at his cell phone and sighs.

"Aren't you gonna answer it?"

Maxwell shakes his head and grins.

"I'll get it later—besides we're about to take off. Don't want to piss the airline people off—they always get even."

He points to a few of the attendants.

"They run the show."

Diana nods in agreement.

"How have you been? Busted any bad guys lately?"

Maxwell laughs and gestures.

"Got a few actually—mostly crimes involving a husband or wife trying to rub each other out using a hit man—and getting caught when the hit man turns out to be an undercover fed."

Diana leans toward Maxwell again.

"Do you have handcuffs?"

Maxwell grins slyly.

"Uh-huh—and yeah—I'm into rough sex too. Been down quite a few roads with the women I've known—entertaining."

Diana licks her lips and winks at Maxwell.

Page 54

"I'm really looking forward to hooking up with you when we land in St. Thomas—it's been a while since I met a guy who knew how to please a woman—knew what he was doing."

Maxwell wags his finger at her and laughs.

15

"Byron seems to like her—he's been having problems with nannies lately—didn't like being bossed around—has issues."

Pamela Henderson turns to look at Astrid.

"I think it's that boy he's been hanging out with. Niels Anderssen is trouble—mentally troubled—no restrictions are placed on him by his parents—that boy is headed for a life of crime as soon as he turns thirteen—seen his type before."

Astrid gives her mother a cautious look.

"I agree—but until I can find a way to keep them apart there's not much I can do about it—believe me I've tried."

Pamela gives Astrid a knowing look.

16
University of the Virgin Islands

"I already told you—I'm not into your sister. She's not my type. I've already moved on since last week. We're over."

Omar Cortez seems annoyed as he walks back and forth in front of his car parked just outside the campus. He stops.

"Uh-huh—tell your sister it was nice while it lasted but I've found someone else—and I suggest she do the same."

He runs his fingers through his hair.

"So what if I popped her—someone had to—she should be thanking me—making her a woman and letting her see what sex between a man and woman can be like courtesy of my dick."

He laughs and gestures with his hand.

"This conversation is over."

He shuts off his cell phone and sighs.

"That stupid jerk is trying my last nerve today."

"I warned you about Cindy Creele. She's gonna be after you from now on—taking her virginity has consequences."

Omar turns around to look at Colin Rossmore and sighs. He seems upset as he watches Colin wagging his finger.

"I never promised her anything other than a good time would be had. She knew my rep. Every girl on campus knows how I roll—I've fucked most of the girls here already—and make no apologies for how I live. She'll just have to deal with it."

Colin reaches out to push Omar.

"Uh-huh—her brother isn't someone you should be messing with Omar. He's busted a few jaws in his time—spends plenty hours at the gym—could easily snap you like a twig."

Omar laughs and looks at his cell phone.

"Steve Creele isn't in any position to lecture me on my behavior with his sister. That frigging dude has slept with plenty of his fellow classmates—many of which I bedded as well."

Colin pushes Omar again.

"We'll see how that works out for you."

He turns to face the golf course across the street and seems pleased at the scenic view. He faces Omar again.

"How about we take up golf?"

Omar laughs.

"Golf is for dorks—besides it's not a real sport anyway if truth be told. Much the same way that fishing isn't really a sport either—seriously—who thinks sitting for hours waiting for a fish to grab hold of bait at the end of a hook is a sport. Uh-huh—real sports requires skill. Fishing and golf requires neither. Ugh."

Colin laughs and shakes his fist at Omar.

"I dare you to say that in public."

Omar makes a lewd gesture at Colin.

17
Nickerson Driveway

"Let it go—Isabel Black is a pathetic virgin. She wishes she were you. Bryce must be desperate if he wants to pop her."

Cliff Nickerson makes a lewd gesture with his hand as he pulls Wendy toward him. He kisses her and grins broadly.

"Nevertheless if Isabel wants war—then I say we give it to her—crush her once and for all—make her see the light."

Wendy giggles as she strokes Cliff's cheek.

"I think we should start a rumor—spread it around that she's been having sex with random college guys—make everyone think she's a slut—her reputation will be ruined—people talk."

Cliff pins Wendy against his car and grins.

"I want you so badly right now."

Wendy glances at Cliff's house and sighs loudly.

"What about your grandparents?"

Cliff shrugs and grins.

"I don't know. Who cares? We can get into my room through the window—they'll never know. My room is at the end of the house—theirs is on the other side—how about it?"

Wendy watches as a grin spreads across Cliff's face. He begins to unbuckle his belt and points toward the house.

"I've got plenty of condoms in my room."

Wendy looks at the house again and seems upset.

"Isabel said you were hanging around Antilles looking for girls—she said you were playing me—said I was a fool."

Cliff clenches his fist and shakes it.

"That stupid whore better watch her mouth if she knows what's good for her—no one likes a frigid gossipy bitch."

Wendy notices his anger and pulls away.

"I didn't believe what she said—told her so too."

Cliff grins and looks at his house again.

"I'm definitely gonna teach that damn bitch a lesson for lying about me behind my back—an eye for an eye deal."

He laughs and pulls Wendy toward him again.

18

"I think you'll do just fine—hope you like living up here in the hills above town—quite the view of Hassel Island."

Page 57

Savannah nods as she takes a sip of tea. She faces Astrid sitting across from her and then turns to face the harbor.

"It's fine—like a living postcard."

Astrid seems pleased and stands up.

"Byron has a friend named Niels. I want you to keep an eye on him whenever he comes by—he's a bit unstable."

Savannah gives Astrid a curious look.

"What do you mean?"

Astrid looks at the glass of tea in her hand.

"He is a magnet for trouble—plays by a different set of rules—and I don't want Byron doing anything stupid."

Savannah nods as Astrid notices her mother shooting her a cautious look. She seems upset and turns away.

19

Windward Passage Hotel

"That stupid brother of mine is in for a rude awakening once we meet. With him out of the way I get everything."

Silas Bell clenches his fists.

"His frigging kid must be dealt with also."

He laughs as he picks up a gun lying nearby on the coffee table. He slowly slides his finger over the trigger and smirks.

"No loose ends left with them lying in the morgue after I take them both out—it'll all be mine—to spend as I please."

He kisses the gun and grins broadly.

20

Smythe Apartment

"You didn't tell me she was pretty. She could have been a model if she'd wanted—looks a lot like **Brooke Shields**."

John Smythe gives his girlfriend a knowing look as she comes toward him holding a book in her hands. He sighs.

"Yeah, I guess so—don't really know her actually. We just spoke a few times—she seemed really nice—adventurous."

Page **58**

Shirley Lindstrom seems confused.

"What does that mean?"

John laughs and gestures with his hand.

"Sandra King told me she liked hiking in the mountains and sailing—said she wasn't the type of girl that cared much for living in front of a mirror like other girls—enjoyed being real."

Shirley walks over to John.

"Are you trying to tell me something?"

John seems nervous and sighs.

"Nothing—nothing at all—just telling you what kind of person Sandra was when she interviewed me for the book."

Shirley watches as John slowly stands and walks over to a small kitchenette. He stands motionless for a few seconds.

"I got the distinct impression that what happened to her on the island left an impact—made her appreciate life."

Shirley stands and walks over to the kitchenette.

"I don't know how she handled it—how *they* handled what happened to them. I'm pretty sure I would've freaked."

John reaches out to put his arms around Shirley. He kisses her and pulls her closer to him. He kisses her again.

"I feel the same way—first having the yacht they were on go down in flames—then to be pursued by sharks—and then to end up in an uncharted island inhabited by the grandsons of a deranged killer. Sounds like one of those movies they released directly to video in the 1990s—the ones where the only thing worse than the script was the really bad acting by actors who couldn't get jobs on TV anymore—not even commercials."

Shirley laughs and jabs John.

"Thank God they stopped making those sorts of movies. They were the worse—such terrible acting and directing."

John playfully wags his finger at Shirley.

"They still make those types of movies—but they usually air on Lifetime before ending up on YouTube for free."

John reaches out to stroke Shirley's hair.

"I'm glad you took a chance on me—said yes when I asked you out. I was dealing with a dry spell and had no confidence."

Shirley kisses John lightly on the lips.

"I should be thanking you—every guy I met wanted to bed me—you were different—you actually wanted to have dinner."

John laughs as he glances at the kitchen sink.

"It took me a while to work up the nerve to suggest you and I spend the night together. I was scared you'd laugh."

Shirley seems about to cry and hugs John warmly. They hug for several seconds. He pulls away suddenly and shrugs.

"Your mother liked me right away—thought I was a funny guy—liked my dry sense of humor—told you I was sweet."

Shirley points her finger at John.

"Uh-huh—and you milked that for quite some time—never let me forget that my mother liked you—bragged about it."

John grins broadly.

"Admit it—you're sweet on me."

Shirley pushes John against the refrigerator.

"I'll admit no such thing."

John pulls Shirley toward him.

"I say otherwise—I say you love me—I know it and you know it—your mother knows it too—said so several times."

Shirley points her finger at John again.

"My mother has a big mouth."

John grabs his cell phone.

"Should I tell her you said that?"

Shirley gives John a cautious look.

"Don't you dare—your ego is already out of control as it is—don't need my mother putting any more ideas into your head and making you even more confident than you already are."

John puts his cell phone down on the counter nearby and wraps his arms around Shirley's waist. He grins broadly.

"I'm really happy—I like being your boyfriend—having you sleeping next to me at night—keeping me grounded."

Tears begin streaming down Shirley's cheeks. John seems confused. He pulls away from Shirley. She turns away. He tries to reach out to her but Shirley pushes him away several times.

"Was it something I said? I'm sorry."

Shirley turns to face John again.

"Why do you always have to say the sweetest things to me—make me love you even more than I already do—make me want you in my life forever—damn you John Smythe."

John laughs as Shirley reacts.

"Like shoot me already."

He gestures at her and they hug again.

21

Peterborg Peninsula

"It's hard to believe a place this beautiful can be so treacherous—heard plenty scary tales from the locals."

Greg gives Ava a strange look as he glances at the used condom in his hand. He tosses it out the window and sighs.

"I don't put much stock into what the locals say—lots of stories they tell are just to scare people away. I have it on good authority this is a favorite spot to fuck—secluded and quiet."

Ava pushes Greg away from her and points.

"I'll just bet—exactly how many girls have you brought out here and fucked—inquiring minds would like to know."

Greg grins broadly and begins laughing.

"I forget—I don't keep track."

Ava jabs Greg.

"Translated into English it means you've fucked so many girls out here you can't remember—probably dozens I bet."

Greg begins putting on his jeans and smirks.

"I'm not saying one way or the other."

He slowly steps out of the car.

"Seriously, I wonder how many ships went down in those waters in front of us—bet there were probably hundreds—since the time **Francis Drake** first sailed through this area."

Ava gets out of Greg's car and sighs.

"Since when did you become a history buff?"

Greg laughs loudly and faces Ava.

"I'm much more than just a guy with a huge dick."

Page **61**

Ava reaches for her blouse and wags her finger at Greg.

"Says who—you're known only for getting every girl in our school to spread their legs—and a few of their mothers too."

Greg makes a lewd gesture with his hand.

"That reminds me—your mother called me earlier—said you were spending too much time with me—seemed pissed."

Ava watches as he begins pulling on his T-shirt.

"Fuck my mother—I still haven't forgiven her for sleeping with my camp counselor last year—played my dad for a fool."

Greg walks toward several large rocks and turns around.

"I think your dad was relieved actually—everyone knows he would rather spend time on his sailboat with Dane Prine."

Ava seems insulted and comes toward Greg.

"Don't you go there—my dad isn't gay."

Greg sticks his finger into his mouth and gags.

"So says you—but Dane is definitely gay—rumors all over town about his escapades at Saddles Bar. Dude can't seem to keep his pants zipped up long enough—spends more time on top of guys than he works—and now he's hanging with your dad on his sailboat. What do you think they're doing below decks?"

Ava angrily grabs Greg's arm.

"Take that back—Dane is just a friend—nothing more."

Greg jerks free of Ava's grip and laughs.

"Uh-huh—a friend with benefits from what I hear—face it your dad is putting out for that loser—giving it up like candy."

Ava grabs Greg's arm again.

"Like you can talk—how many skanky girls have you fucked in the last week—people talk about you too—you've got quite the rep with older women too—lots of repeat visits."

Greg licks his lips and laughs.

"That's right—but at least I like girls."

Ava reacts as if she's been stung and releases her grip on Greg's arm. He faces the ocean again and grins broadly.

"How about we catch a movie?"

Ava gives Greg a nasty look.

"I want to go home. I'm done with you."

He laughs as he watches her walk back toward the car and makes a lewd gesture with his finger as she stops suddenly.

"I guess tomorrow isn't gonna happen?"

Ava purposely ignores Greg and gets into the car.

22
Estate Mafolie

"I want to take down that miserable gossiping bitch."

Cliff clenches his fist and turns to look at Marco Verde as they sit in a car just outside the entrance of a private road leading to very expensive designer homes behind wrought iron gates.

"Forget about Isabel Black, OK. That girl isn't going to give it up to the likes of you. Your rep has been stained plenty."

Cliff rolls his eyes knowingly.

"Ugh—I don't want to date her—I just want to fuck her. Take her down a path of no return—then throw her aside. Show her how much power I have over her once she's been played."

He makes a lewd gesture with his finger.

"You are my ace in the hole—she tutors you two days a week. Get her to go out with me—I'll take it from there."

Marco seems uneasy and shrugs.

"I don't know about this cracked idea of yours. If you try to bang her she'll cry rape—tell the cops she said no. Girls like her aren't very forgiving when they get popped by guys like you."

Cliff shoves his fist in Marco's face.

"You owe me—I got you a date with Lena Victor."

Marco gives Cliff a disgusted look.

"Uh-huh—but she wouldn't let me get into her panties because of what you did—said she and you already knew each other really well—and that she was through spreading her legs for every guy that wanted a piece—demanded we date first."

Cliff playfully jabs Marco.

"How was I to know she'd suddenly get all **Bette Davis** on me and hold out for something more respectful? Seriously, I tried but you just have bad luck—chicks just don't dig you at all."

Marco turns away and seems upset. He sighs loudly.

"I've never had a problem with girls before—at least not until lately anyway—thanks to you and others like you—fucking every girl you meet pretending you like them—then ignoring them after you get what you want—making every guy on this island seem like they only want one thing and one thing only."

Cliff begins laughing hysterically.

"What are you gonna do now? Start bawling?"

He jabs Marco again and makes a lewd gesture with his finger as he turns to look at the entrance of the gated driveway.

"Listen—I want Isabel Black added to my long list of conquests—and you're gonna help me score with that bitch. Once I pop her she'll never be able to say squat about me again."

Marco turns to look at the cemetery across the street adjacent to a small elementary school. He seems upset.

"I used to go to that school when I was little—after school a few of us kids would all go into the cemetery and look at headstones. Pretend the place was haunted—act like the bodies buried in the above-ground tombs walked around at night."

Cliff glances at the cemetery and at Marco.

"I don't believe in ghosts."

He waves his hand in the air.

"If I can't see it I don't believe it. It's that simple."

Marco looks at the cemetery again.

"I never said it was haunted—I only said my classmates and I pretended that it was. Nevertheless you'd never catch me walking around in there at night—place is seriously creepy."

Cliff grabs Marco by the shoulders.

"What about Isabel Black?"

Marco seems uneasy and nods.

23
Windward Passage Hotel

"Did you see the look on that woman's face when she realized what you and I were doing? She was shocked."

Page **64**

Maxwell grins as he watches Diana open the door to her hotel room. She gestures him inside and closes the door.

"I thought that tightly-wound old biddy was going to have a heart attack knowing we were part of the mile-high club."

Maxwell wags his finger at Diana.

"I'm not sorry we did what we did—we both needed to release some pent-up energy—it was quite enjoyable."

He watches as she walks toward a mini bar.

"How about a drink—and then we head off toward the bedroom and make use of the bed—spend the night?"

Diana grins broadly.

"I got no problem with that."

Maxwell walks over toward the window. He stands there a couple of minutes marveling at the view of Hassel Island.

24
Frenchman's Reef Resort

"I can't believe we're all going to be together again after what happened—it just seemed so unreal at the time."

Victoria de Hoya walks toward Scott and Sandra with a tray ladled with several wine glasses and a few snacks.

"It took me a while to process everything that happened to us on that island—and then there was the coverage."

She laughs as she sits down next to Sandra.

"We were treated as if we were movie stars—cameras were everywhere—reporters hung on our every word."

Scott waves his hand in the air.

"I loved every minute of it—the coverage—not what happened. It took weeks for the truth to emerge about what had been taking place on that island for decades. But there are still things that remain unclear about Zaroff and his vile brood."

Sandra points her finger at Scott.

"I tried my best researching everything I found out—but there were things they did that are still unknown—of course what happened to Tristan Montgomery Bell remains a mystery."

Page **65**

Scott takes a swig of wine and laughs.

"That old coot went down with his yacht. There's no other explanation concerning the conclusion to his story. He's lying at the bottom of the ocean somewhere in the deep blue sea."

Sandra grabs Scott's arm.

"I was never able to find out what set him off except that it had something to do with Wesley Mayfield. From what I found out Mayfield was working for some shady mob types out of San Francisco that had a grudge against Bell for some reason."

Scott finishes the wine in his glass and smirks.

"Wesley Mayfield—now that was a character. That dude was seriously unpleasant to come across—viciously rude."

Victoria looks at Scott curiously.

"Have you seen Armand Bell yet?"

Scott shakes his head.

"He's coming to the signing."

Sandra turns to face Victoria and sighs.

"I'm sorry Laura can't make it."

Victoria waves her hand in the air.

"She just couldn't handle it. She's been in therapy."

Victoria pours herself another drink.

"Diana Munroe is coming. She called earlier and said she was on her way. She's been a good friend to Laura."

Sandra and Scott look at each other.

"Maxwell Pendergraft is coming too. He's staying at the same hotel we're staying at. He'll be pleased to see you."

Victoria smiles broadly.

25

Shirley is blindfolded as John cautiously guides her toward the sofa. He gently helps her sit down and carefully takes the blindfold off as she looks at the collection of painting supplies.

"These are for you—thought that since you like painting so much you should have your own starter kit instead of the used one that dinky art school supplies you with every weekend."

Page 66

Shirley reaches out to hug John warmly.

"You're just so sweet—the most wonderful boyfriend a girl like me could ever want—*Prince Charming*—I love you."

John wags his finger at her.

"I expect to see sunsets and beaches."

He laughs as she hugs him again.

"Magens Bay is a definite painting waiting to happen in the next week or so—followed by Stumpy Bay Beach."

Shirley gives John a knowing look.

"Uh-huh—I see where this is going concerning your two favorite locations on this island. Bribery is in play."

John begins laughing and reaches out to hug Shirley for a few seconds. He looks at her and seems pleased. He grins.

"I've always got a motive for everything."

Shirley pretends to slap John.

26

"I think you should come back to Los Angeles with me after the book signing. Laura would really like it if you did."

Maxwell pulls Diana toward him and smirks.

"What about you? Would you like it?"

Diana reaches out to stroke Maxwell's chest.

"What do you think?"

They begin kissing passionately.

TO BE CONTINUED

A Brief Look at the Third Episode

A visitor from the past unnerves Armand while a surprise encounter gives Maxwell plenty to think about concerning his future as a botched kidnapping attempt goes terribly wrong.

Episode 3
Innocence Lost

1
Verde Driveway

"Uh-huh—like I said, I still need more help with that history essay from last week. How about we meet tomorrow?"

Marco Verde shakes his head several times as he turns to look at the driveway leading to his home. He sighs loudly.

"Of course I'll pay. Haven't I always?"

He runs his fingers through his hair and shrugs.

"Great—I'll see you tomorrow at ten."

He nods several times and shuts off his cell phone.

"I don't like this one bit."

He turns to face Cliff Nickerson.

"This will end badly."

Cliff points his finger at Marco and laughs.

"That bitch had it coming. When I'm done with her there'll be no turning back—she'll just be one of my girls—old news."

Marco grimaces.

"This is just wrong—I won't do it."

Cliff grabs Marco by his neck. He shoves him.

"You'll do it—or I'll make your life a living hell. Make you wish you'd never been born—destroy your reputation."

Marco and Cliff stare at each other for a few seconds as Cliff pulls out his cell phone. He grins broadly. Marco looks at the cell phone and then at Cliff. Cliff watches Marco's reaction as he brings forward a video. They look at each other. Cliff smirks.

"Don't fuck with me or I'll be forced to let this nasty little video you made with Alicia Penn be uploaded to YouTube."

Marco reacts and seems in shock.

"How did you get—only Alicia and I had a copy?"

Cliff grins broadly and begins laughing.

"Let's just say she gave it up willingly once my dick was inside her—believed me when I said I only wanted to see it to improve my technique after making her think your skills in the sack were the envy of every guy on this island. Ugh—women are stupid—she fell for that load and handed it over. I copied it and now you and I will play ball where Isabel Black is concerned."

He pushes Marco against his car and grins.

"You pick your poison—delivering Isabel to me on a silver platter or having everyone find out you barely knew your way between Alicia's legs. Imagine how that kind of news will be received. It'll be the end of your social life—total disaster."

He released his grip on Marco's neck.

"I'll expect results soon."

He winks at Marco.

"Or everyone will know how much of a dud in bed you are—how much experience you don't have with girls."

He walks to his car as Marco seems unable to move.

2

Back Street Gallery

"I didn't expect to see you again today? I thought you said you needed time—wanted to make sure? Figure things out?"

Ingrid de Hoya closes the front door behind her and faces Jordan McKinney as he comes toward her. She sighs loudly.

Page **70**

"I was wrong—just got a lecture from my friend about how stupid I was acting about dating you—said you were a catch."

Jordan grins broadly and seems amused.

"I guess I owe Allegra. Regardless, she's right by the way. I *am* a catch without a doubt—no baggage and only a handful of ex-girlfriends to speak of—no crazy exes out for my scalp."

Ingrid wags a finger at Jordan.

"Did she just call you?"

Jordan grins broadly again and nods.

"Uh-huh—said you wanted to get into my pants."

Ingrid reacts and seems embarrassed.

"I'll wring her neck—I swear I will."

Jordan laughs.

"You'll do no such thing—except to thank her. I'm quite pleased by the turn of events—willing to have dinner."

Ingrid gives Jordan a knowing look. She circles him and watches as he grins broadly again. He points to the front door.

"I'm almost done for the day—I'm open for us having a quiet dinner at my condo on Bunker Hill. Open for you to tell me how much you like me—how much you've imagined me naked right before you seduce me—right before I surrender."

Ingrid wags her finger at Jordan again.

"Seems Allegra and I are gonna have a very long talk about what is and what isn't true—oh yeah, she's so dead."

Jordan laughs and pulls Ingrid toward him.

"She had every right—she only wants what I want—for you to be happy—to be involved with a decent guy—*me*."

Jordan gestures with his hand and laughs.

Two Days Later

3

Havensight Mall Bookshop

"Exactly what I was thinking—we'll have customers come toward the table and then exit on the right—simple—fast."

Sandra King seems confused and sighs loudly as she looks at Cassandra Covington. She watches as Cassandra turns to face the bookstore owner seconds later. They exchange glances.

"We can expect plenty of passengers to stop by once they've disembarked. They love this mall—very popular."

Sandra nods as Cassandra pulls Maggie Rios aside and points to the door. She singles out several posters and sighs.

"Those might have to come down until after the signing has concluded. The cover of Sandra's book should be the only thing people can see from the sidewalk—create demand."

Maggie turns to look at Sandra and then at Cassandra once more as a few customers walk past them. She grimaces.

4
Mountain Top

"You should be so lucky—I whipped your ass fair and square—wiped that silly grin off your face—not prepared."

Scott Malone jabs Maxwell Pendergraft as they head toward Maxwell's car. Maxwell stops and faces Scott.

"You cheated—you waited until I wasn't looking and then played your game—pathetic—you should be ashamed."

Scott begins laughing.

"It's your own fault I whipped you. No one told you to turn and look at that woman at the ice cream stand. Admit it—I got you because your mind was focusing on another conquest."

Maxwell turns to look at the tennis courts again and laughs as he opens the door to his car. He grins broadly.

"Got a date with her tonight—her place—made it clear that I bring plenty of condoms—made some vile threats."

He makes a lewd gesture with his finger.

"She said I would be seriously tired when she was done with me. Let me know I would be unable to move afterwards."

Scott rolls his eyes and gets into the car.

"I wonder what she's gonna do when you disappoint her royally—women take being slighted in bed personally."

Page **72**

Maxwell shakes his fist at Scott and grins.

"I've never had complaints—only accolades from my many admirers. Women can't get enough of my handsome face."

Scott pretends to be disgusted. He makes a gagging gesture with his hand. Maxwell shakes his fist again.

"I bet Sandra is on pins and needles thinking about the signing tomorrow. I would be if I were her—lots of pressure."

Scott waves his hand in the air.

"Her publisher is probably wishing for every copy to sell at the signing—Sandra said they printed about fifty thousand."

Maxwell starts the car and as he drives toward the main road from the tennis courts he turns to face Scott and sighs.

"Is it still hard when you remember what happened on that island? Diana said she still has terrible nightmares."

Scott runs his fingers through his hair.

"I still think about it—Sandra too for that matter—but it's gotten better as time has gone by—the six of us are in a club that no one wants to join—not even for a day—but we were dealt the hand we got and somehow made it through in one piece."

He runs his fingers through his hair again.

"Victoria said Laura has been in therapy for a while now. Said she hasn't been the same since—remembers too much."

Maxwell wipes sweat from his brow.

"When I first got to the island and saw firsthand what had taken place, it was like living someone else's life. I couldn't even fathom how you guys survived. The island reeked of death—so many mummified bodies inside that mansion. Zaroff and his grandsons destroyed so many lives. Once it was all over and we had indentified the remains—the hardest part was yet to come. It was torture calling each and every one of the relatives and letting them know that at long last their missing loved ones would finally be able to rest in peace. Of course there were a few that were unable to be indentified even through DNA. One day perhaps."

Maxwell watches the reaction on Scott's face.

"I hear that some Hollywood producer has been trying to get Sandra's attention—called her publisher several times."

Page **73**

Maxwell looks at the steering wheel and at the narrow road in front of him. He shakes his head several times.

"I got a friend in Los Angeles that makes movies. His name is Wesley Madison—got quite a story himself."

Scott reacts and snaps his fingers.

"That's the producer that's been calling us endlessly about wanting to produce Sandra's book—quite tenacious."

Maxwell begins laughing.

"That sounds like Wesley without a doubt. That kid doesn't know when to quit—got himself into a world of trouble a few years back in a little town in Maine called Marble Hills."

Maxwell pulls the car to a stop.

"He was headed down the path of no return—a long stay in the slammer—until he found out his entire life had been a lie. It was quite the tabloid grabber. Young Madison found out his real father was a soap opera actor amid the backdrop of a deranged serial killer running amok for several months. The newspapers in Boston had a field day with both stories. The truth was even more shocking than anything Hollywood could write—Jennifer Parker was a character that even the best actresses today would find hard to play—killed several of her classmates in a fit of rage."

Scott seems confused and sighs.

"I know the *story*—Jennifer Parker was the niece of my boss. Roland Parker me she was always a bit unstable when she was a kid—spent a few years at a mental hospital if I recall."

Maxwell wags his finger at Scott.

"Parker must be quite a character himself. Heard he's a real ball-buster—doesn't make things easy for anyone."

Scott stifles a laugh.

"He's tough—but fair. I've fucked-up so many times and he still takes me back—can't fire me even if he wanted to. He tried to play it tough after what happened at the island—but I could see he was really worried about me—kept asking if I needed a vacation—seemed concerned I would need therapy."

Maxwell jabs Scott playfully.

"What about Sandra? Is she adjusting?"

Scott gestures with his hand.

"I assume—we don't talk about what happened on a regular basis—so many other things has happened since."

Maxwell nods in agreement and sighs.

"Tell me about it—plenty of things that shouldn't be treaded upon—especially with Marble Hills—loose ends."

Scott shoots Maxwell a curious look.

"Is this about the old man who killed himself?"

Maxwell shakes his head.

"No—it was something else—a weird situation to say the least—saw something—can't talk about it—hard to explain."

Scott grabs Maxwell's arm.

"Can't or won't? There is a difference."

Maxwell turns away.

"I can't talk about what can't be rationally explained."

Maxwell wipes sweat from his brow again.

5
Coki Beach

"I already told you I know what I have to do. She doesn't suspect anything. Stop worrying—trust me—believe."

Savannah Windsor walks back and forth among several large trees as she talks on her cell phone. She sighs loudly.

"I said I could handle it and I'm handling it."

She turns to look as Byron Blakely comes toward her from the surf. Behind him is Pamela Henderson looking a bit tired as she reaches the picnic table. Savannah smiles and faces them.

"How was the water?"

Pamela points toward Byron.

"That one thinks he's a fish—kept swimming farther and farther against the tide—another **Michael Phelps**."

Savannah immediately shoots Byron a sharp look as she shuts off her cell phone. She points her finger at the little boy.

"I thought we talked about this already—got to be careful whenever you go in the water—be wary of everything."

Page 75

Byron rolls his eyes and turns to face the ocean.

"I've got it down perfectly—I can swim better than most kids my age—I'm not afraid—I know exactly what I'm doing."

Savannah and Pamela look at each other.

"Uh-huh—so you say—but I'm still going to tell your mother what you did—let her know you didn't listen."

Byron seems upset and sighs.

"You're no fun at all—crashing my party every time I want to do something really exciting for a change. Niels says."

Savannah and Pamela look at each other again.

"Niels doesn't know everything there is to know about life—he just thinks he does—thinks he's an expert."

Byron makes a lewd gesture with his finger and yawns.

"This conversation is boring me."

Pamela reacts and grabs Byron by the arm.

6
Denmark Hill

"Forget it—I'm not interested."

Isabel Black angrily slams the door shut to Marco's car. He watches as she turns around and comes toward him.

"He only wants one thing from a girl."

Marco jumps out of his car.

"He's really nice when you get to know him."

Isabel rolls her eyes.

"Uh-huh—I'll just bet—until he gets what he wants and then he doesn't know you any longer—his rep speaks."

Marco grabs Isabel's arm.

"Cliff is one of the good guys if truth be told. He just wants to go on a date—nothing more—he'll be a gentleman."

Isabel jerks free of Marco's grip.

"Cliff Nickerson is a lot of things but a gentleman he's not. He uses every girl he dates—scores and then dumps them."

Marco runs his fingers through his hair.

"Are you saying you won't go out with him?"

Isabel makes a lewd gesture with her finger.

"Not even if my life depended on it."

She watches Marco's reaction and sighs loudly.

"This conversation is over."

She glances at the steps leading to her home several feet away. Marco runs his fingers through his hair again.

"Cliff isn't going to like being slighted."

Isabel begins to laugh.

"Do I look like I care?"

Marco grabs his cell phone.

"Well, for the record I think you're making a mistake. He expected you to say yes—to see him in a different light."

Isabel shakes her head and turns away.

"That will never happen—he disgusts me."

Marco seems upset as he watches her walk toward the entrance of her home. He shakes his head several times.

7

Mafolie Hotel

Scott slowly closes the door behind him and turns to face Maxwell. They look at each other curiously for a few seconds.

"Earlier you mentioned something happened while you were in Marble Hills dealing with what Roland's niece did."

Maxwell winces and faces the balcony.

"Not much to tell actually. It's over."

Scott walks over to where Maxwell is standing.

"Uh-huh—sure it is—that freaky look on your face said plenty—you seemed pretty shook up about something."

Maxwell points his finger at Scott.

"Are you looking for your next story?"

Scott rolls his eyes.

"Is there a story? I was just trying to understand what you meant earlier by such a statement. What else happened in that little town? From what you implied I got the impression there was something else—a separate story—seriously complicated."

Page **77**

Maxwell jabs Scott in the chest and walks toward the balcony. Scott follows him seconds later. He gestures.

"Well, was there something else that happened that no one knew about, Maxwell? Something that years later you still can't face without acting like you saw a ghost or something."

Maxwell grimaces and wrings his hand.

8
Garden Street

"I told you she wouldn't go for it. She thinks you're beneath her. Said she'd never let you score—hates you."

Cliff grabs Marco's arm in a rage.

"That bitch is gonna pay dearly for daring to ignore my request. Uh-huh—she'll be beneath me soon enough in the backseat of my car while I fuck her endlessly. How dare her."

Marco gives Cliff a knowing look.

"What are you planning to do to Isabel?"

Cliff grins broadly and shakes his fist in the air.

"She'll see the light really soon—see that I'm not someone she can trifle with—and when I'm done with her there'll be no way for her to show her face in public again. Damn that bitch."

He points his finger at Marco.

"I have a plan—and you're gonna help me."

Marco seems upset.

"I want no part of this—Isabel's father is a lawyer—sends people to jail—leave me out of whatever schemes you're thinking of enacting to even the score with Isabel Black. I'm done."

Cliff begins laughing loudly.

"You're done when I say you're done."

He clenches his fist.

"I can get pretty angry when I don't get what I want from someone that owes me—especially if that person happens to be you. It would be a shame if you were to have an accident."

Marco watches as a grin spreads across Cliff's face while he clenches his fist several times. Marco sighs loudly and nods.

Page 78

"No wonder you don't have any friends."

Cliff throws his head back and laughs as he jabs Marco in the chest. He pulls out a pair of brass knuckles from the back pocket of his Levi's. He gives Marco a knowing look.

"Don't need any friends when I have these—they do my talking for me—seems to me you'd better think about that the next time you talk back to me and say you won't do what I ask of you—knowing you have no choice on account I own you."

Marco gives Cliff a nasty look and sighs.

9
Reynolds Estate

"Hello brother."

Armand Bell seems in shock as he looks at the man staring at him with a huge grin. Silas Bell gestures with his hand.

"Well, aren't you going to invite me inside?"

Armand continues to stand motionless for several more seconds before Silas extends his hand. Armand sighs.

"What are you doing here?"

Silas grins slyly.

"What a question to ask your brother?"

Armand shrugs.

"Uh-huh—a brother who tried to kill me and my mother with poisonous spiders—claimed you didn't realize they were toxic to humans. Yeah, how about we talk about that?"

Silas grimaces and snaps his fingers.

"I was a kid—let it go already."

Armand wipes sweat from his brow.

"You were nineteen—hardly a kid in the eyes of the law in Australia—they knew what you were capable of—wanted to toss you in a mental hospital—but *he* refused to put you away."

Silas shakes his fist at Armand.

"*He* as you call him—was our father—knew that I didn't mean anything by it—just wanted to scare you silly—a prank and nothing more. I came all this way to see—I was hoping."

Page **79**

Armand continues standing in the doorway.

"Some mistakes can't be ignored—especially if they weren't mistakes at all—but were intentions. I think it would be best if you leave. I don't have a brother—half or otherwise."

Silas angrily clenches his fist.

"Fuck you—it's clear you're still the same stuck-up little prick you were all those years ago—no wonder father cast you aside—he couldn't deal with a son that was a chump—a wimp with no guts—one that thinks he's better than everyone else."

Silas turns away and stops. He grins broadly.

"It would be such a crying shame if the truth came out about your mother—and what *really* happened years ago."

He turns away as Armand seems confused.

10

Scott hands Maxwell a can of beer and turns to look at the view of Charlotte Amalie before them. He grins broadly.

"So, are you gonna tell me or not?"

Maxwell takes a swig of beer.

"Tell you what?"

Scott reaches out to jab Maxwell.

"Tell me about what you alluded to earlier about Marble Hills and some weird situation that happened there—besides the string of murders which brought you to that peaceful little hamlet in the first place? Did you see a UFO? Got probed by little green men? Or did you find out that witches are real? Do tell—*spill*."

Maxwell wags his finger at Scott.

"Nice try—but there's nothing to talk about—I said that something happened—I never said it was a major event."

He grins broadly and stifles a laugh.

"Not everything can be explained—and not everything should be explained—some things are best left unexplained."

Scott rolls his eyes and takes a swig of beer.

"Uh-huh—so you say Maxwell—but from what I saw by the look on your face it was something major—left an impact."

Maxwell playfully shakes his fist at Scott.

"I'm done with this conversation."

Scott gives Maxwell a curious look as he takes another swig of beer. He faces the city of Charlotte Amalie again.

"This island is full of stories too—all sorts of weird things have happened here. Plenty of rampant tales of pirates, voodoo and werewolves—the locals swear by it. Never a dull moment if you find the right person willing to tell you that one of their dead relatives had encounters with werewolves—and zombies."

Maxwell shakes his head and smirks.

"You forgot about vampires? Did the locals have stories about the undead dancing in cemeteries at midnight?"

Scott shoots Maxwell a cautious look.

"Mock me all you want—but New England isn't the only place where people can't let go of their past—the Virgin Islands has had plenty of tragedy—the land is stained with blood."

Maxwell pats Scott on the shoulder.

"I wasn't mocking you—just trying to lighten the moment a bit—get us past the morbid curiosity you seem to have all of a sudden because of something I said in passing—just deal."

Scott waves his hand in the air.

"Can't fault a guy for trying to come up with his next story especially after how dull the last few weeks have been. Nothing happening with the exception of a few celebrities getting into trouble with their parole officers—thought you might have been able to lead me to something interesting concerning that little town where the tabloid press had a field day a few years back."

Maxwell runs his fingers through his hair.

11

Mandahl Bay Beach

"When do we grab the kid? Did your sister tell you when she and the brat will come by? I hope she knows what to do."

Brent Crawford grabs Derek Ving by the shoulder and jerks him backwards. They look at each other. Brent sighs.

Page **81**

"Savannah is on schedule—she's bringing Byron over tomorrow. No one knows about this place. Place is usually deserted most of the time—locals dread it for some reason."

Derek gives Brent a knowing look.

"I still think your sister will unravel and mess things up for us—the cops will be watching her afterwards—waiting."

Brent begins laughing at Derek.

"I'm aware of how the local cops work their game—but there's nothing to worry about concerning my sister."

He clenches his fist.

"Once I get my hands on that brat all bets are off. Astrid will pay plenty to get him back—and even then—there's no guarantee that kidnappings have happy endings. It would be such a shame if along the way her precious son had an accident and then—he was found dead by the side of a lonely road."

He points toward the sky for a second.

"She's young. She can easily have another kid with that boring guy she's been dating—not a big deal actually."

Derek reacts but says nothing.

12
Back Street Cafe

"I thought you said Warner Brothers wanted to turn my book into a blockbuster movie? Did they change their minds?"

Justin Manslow looks at Sandra and smirks.

"They're still thinking about it."

Sandra seems pleased.

"When do we fly out to Los Angeles?"

Justin waves his hand in the air.

"They optioned it—they didn't buy it. It has to be shopped first—get backers who want to finance it. Other than that there's no way for Warner Brothers to get the backing they'll need."

He points to the door and grins broadly.

"Filming location is gonna be difficult. Mysterious Island is off limits—there's no way they'll be allowed to film there."

Sandra seems confused and lowers her voice.

"Why can't the movie be filmed where it happened?"

Justin runs his fingers through his hair.

"The entire island has been landscaped and turned into a park—wait until you see it later this week. From what I saw it looks completely different than it did before. Lawns and flowers everywhere—millions of dollars were spent to clean it up."

He pulls out a folder and shoves it at Sandra.

"There are other islands just off St. Thomas we can use. Most are completely uninhabited and could double as a filming location. It's the best we'll be able to get—either that or they might opt to film the entire movie on Catalina Island."

Sandra reacts and looks at Justin curiously.

"No way am I going to allow my movie to be filmed off the coast of California—especially with what happened there back in November 1981. Ugh—there's absolutely no way I'll allow it."

Justin looks at the folder and then at Sandra.

"What happened in November 1981?"

Sandra seems upset and sighs.

"**Natalie Wood**."

She leans closer to Justin.

"Her husband **Robert Wagner** pushed her off their boat and the LAPD helped him cover it up. He was a failed movie actor who acted on a few lame television shows. It was hot news back then from what I heard—my mother told me all about it—she loved Natalie. My mother said he killed her because she found out Wagner was gay and he didn't want anyone to know—sad."

Justin rolls his eyes and smirks.

"I'd place bets that the Virgin Islands have had plenty of grisly murders as well—some on those islands I mentioned."

Justin clasps his hands together.

"What's the name of the producer who optioned your book? Do I know him? Has he done anything I've seen?"

Justin looks at the folder.

"Can I talk to him?"

Sandra pulls out her cell phone.

"Your wish is my command."

Justin watches as Sandra rapidly dials several numbers and seconds later the screen on her cell phone suddenly comes alive. Staring back at them is a young man. He smiles broadly.

"Justin Manslow, meet Wesley Madison."

Sandra grins as they acknowledge each other.

13
Mafolie Hotel

Maxwell closes the door behind him and sighs loudly as he walks toward a mini bar several feet away. He hears a sound seconds later. He turns around and sees nothing. He shrugs.

"I must be hearing things."

At that moment a blinding flash occurs. He blinks several times and seems slightly confused as he realizes he's no longer alone in the room. He slowly turns around and reacts.

"Hello Maxwell."

He stands frozen in shock as Tiffany Johnson comes toward where he's standing and points at him accusingly.

"You and I have to talk."

Maxwell runs his fingers through his hair.

"Did something happen?"

She gestures with her hand.

"Expecting Diana Munroe I presume?"

He looks at Tiffany curiously.

"How do you know about Diana Munroe?"

Tiffany rolls her eyes knowingly.

"Are you seriously asking me a question like that?"

He shrugs and watches as she takes a step forward. He rubs his eyes as he seems unsure of what is happening.

"I thought what happened last week in Marble Hills was over—thought the matter had been handled. I assumed."

Tiffany nods and takes another step forward.

"It was—over and done with actually—of course there's another matter to discuss presently—loose lips sinks ships."

Maxwell continues standing silently as his eyes seem riveted to the apparition standing before him. Tiffany sighs.

"It appears you and I have some things to talk about concerning your ability to keep quiet about Glass Owl."

She takes another step forward.

"Scott Malone."

Maxwell runs his fingers through his hair again.

"What about him?"

Tiffany seems annoyed.

"Scott Malone is not to be told."

Maxwell nervously watches as Tiffany takes yet another step forward and stops suddenly. She raises her hand.

"What happened at Glass Owl must remain only between those who were present. I'm sure I don't have to tell you what happened to Gina Bentley after she began telling people she saw me. She was assumed to be a basket case—mentally ill."

Maxwell nods in agreement.

"Understood—I see your point. There will be no more discussions with Scott Malone or anyone about what happened at Glass Owl that day. I'll refrain—you have my word."

Tiffany smiles broadly.

"I know you'd see it my way. Only those who were there will ever know what happened—and what was discussed."

She turns to look at the hotel room.

"For the record—Scott Malone is a good guy. He had some major issues in his youth—but he's turned his life around."

She gestures with her hand.

"He's a worthy friend."

Maxwell nods and seconds later he's alone in the hotel room again. He turns to face the mini bar once more and sighs.

14
Anderssen Estate

"What about it Byron—are you game? Or are you going to chicken out again and pretend you don't know what to do?"

Page **85**

Niels Anderssen walks back and forth in front of a swimming pool made of shiny blue rocks. He stops and sighs.

"Come on already—I told you it would be fun."

He gestures wildly with his hand.

"She'll never suspect anything—we'll be gone before she can figure out what we're up to—adults are really stupid."

He laughs and looks toward his house.

"My parents are fools—I know more than they do."

He gestures again and walks toward a grove of mahogany trees nearby. He leans against one of the trees and smirks.

"Trust me—it'll be fun."

Byron rolls his eyes and sighs loudly.

15
Los Angeles

"Uh-huh—yeah—I've produced a few films already—one for Netflix last year and three the year before for Sony."

Wesley leans back in his chair as he looks at Sandra and Justin on the screen of his computer. He grins broadly.

"How is the weather out there? I bet it's perfect all year round—sun and fun every day of the week—like a postcard."

He watches Sandra as she reacts with a knowing grin.

"I haven't been to the beach yet—too busy."

Wesley leans forward.

"Oh, that's too bad—I heard they got spectacular beaches there—like stepping into one of those postcards you find at the airport gift shops when you're about ready to board a flight."

Sandra turns to face Justin.

"My jailer won't let me have any fun."

Wesley grins.

"I'll do justice to your book. I'm gonna hire a really good screenwriter to adapt it the right way—leave the story intact."

He picks up a copy of the book on his desk.

"You lived through something extraordinary that most people couldn't imagine dealing with—starting with me."

Page 86

Sandra gestures with her hand and smiles.

"I had no idea I was living through anything different at the time—I was scared out of my mind that it was all going to end in a bad way. The yacht sinking was bad enough—and dealing with hungry sharks was no picnic either. But the killer brothers were something out of a horror movie—sadistically twisted."

She glances at Justin for a few seconds.

"It still seems like it was all a dream."

Wesley looks at the book again.

"In chapter twelve you said you had no clue there were cameras in the Coast Guard copters streaming live footage—said when you arrived back on St. Thomas you were caught off guard when you saw people standing there cheering—treating you and the others like celebrities. I got the idea you were in shock."

Sandra leans back in her chair.

"I was unaware until I saw hundreds of people waiting for us, acting like they were watching a movie. It was quite a moment realizing what was actually happening in real time. Afterwards when I found out how it all came to be—I had no words."

Wesley looks at his watch.

"I'm meeting with several directors later."

He holds up the book again.

"You'll have final approval of course."

Sandra nods and seems pleased.

"I think I'm going to like working with you."

Wesley grins broadly.

16
Windward Passage Hotel

Silas clenches his fist as he slams the door and walks toward the balcony. He stares at Hassel Island in a distance.

"That frigging bastard is a dead man."

He begins laughing hysterically.

"But first things first—got to make my dear brother feel pain. Uh-huh—and I know how to make that happen—sweet."

He walks over to where a lone suitcase is lying. He grins broadly as he grabs it and throws open the cover. He laughs.

"Accidents happen every day—it seems my dear brother needs to know how it feels to lose his precious offspring."

He grins broadly as he pulls out a small handgun. Silas strokes it gently for a few seconds. His face is wreathed in an evil grin as he turns to face the door. He begins laughing loudly.

"Uh-huh—kids die every day from gunshot wounds to the head—most of the time a family member is to blame."

He begins laughing even louder.

"I would give anything to see the look on my wretched brother's face as he stares at his dead son lying in a casket."

He kisses the handgun several times.

17

"Uh-huh—you heard me right Jasmine—I've hired a personal bodyguard for Trevor and for you. It seems my deranged half-brother decided to pay me a visit earlier. He's certifiable."

He leans against the wall in the kitchen.

"From today you've got to be aware of your surroundings whenever you leave your house. Silas is dangerous—he tried to kill me when I was six. Claimed he didn't know what he was doing. But he did—knew exactly what he was doing—tried twice if you must know the truth. Definitely belongs in a loony bin."

Jasmine Rossmore runs her fingers through her hair as Armand stares at her curiously. She looks away for a few seconds as a child's voice can be heard several feet away. He sighs.

"I'll be in touch later."

Jasmine nods as the screen goes blank. Armand sighs and turns to look at the hallway leading away from the kitchen.

"I guess I should let my mother know that Silas is here in the islands. Tell her to stay in Europe for the time being."

He begins dialing and stops.

"I wonder why he's actually here on St. Thomas. Why did he fly halfway around the world? He must want something."

Page **88**

He turns to look at his cell phone nervously and shrugs.

"The question is what? What is he up to?"

He walks toward an enclosed patio a few feet away and begins dialing again. He waits a few seconds for a response.

18
Blakely Mansion

"I was beginning to think you weren't coming?"

Byron gives Niels a knowing look as he runs from the driveway toward a narrow road. He looks back nervously.

"I told you I would. I'm not a chicken."

Niels rolls his eyes and shrugs.

"Come on—my folks think I'm studying in my room—no way would they assume I'd climb out the window and escape."

He begins laughing loudly.

"Parents are so stupid sometimes."

Byron looks at Niels oddly and nods in agreement seconds later. He seems uneasy as Niels turns to look at the deserted street leading away from the driveway. He grins broadly.

"There's an abandoned park down the road—I heard from the crest you can see Magens Bay on one side and Charlotte Amalie on the other—almost like being on top of the world."

Byron stops and looks around.

"Is there gonna be bugs everywhere? You know—spiders hanging from branches—ready to bite? I hate spiders."

Niels points his finger at Byron.

"It's an old park—deserted—what do you think? Of course there will be bugs—spiders too—bet they'll be pretty big."

Byron reacts. He twitches a little.

"I don't know about this park thing."

Niels seems annoyed and grabs Byron by the arm. He faces the road and grins. Byron jerks free of his friend's grip.

"I've changed my mind."

Niels shakes his fist at Byron and sighs.

"I knew you were a chicken—said it plenty."

Byron looks at Niels for a few seconds and begins walking toward the driveway again. Niels makes a lewd gesture with his finger and slowly begins walking down the narrow road alone.

19
Mafolie Hotel

"I guess your impromptu meeting with Wesley Madison went smoothly—nice that he isn't a jerk—helps a lot."

Sandra rolls her eyes at Scott.

"He was nice—really nice. Wanted me to fly out Los Angeles to meet with him—give input. I said I would."

Scott gives Justin a cautious look.

"Uh-huh—I see I'll have to pay that dude a visit too."

He grins slyly and laughs.

"Make sure he knows his place."

Sandra gives Scott a knowing look.

"You'll do no such thing."

Scott wags his finger at Sandra.

"I will. Count on it."

Sandra glances at Justin and then at Scott.

"I expect you to be on your best behavior if you insist on coming with me—none of that macho guy stuff you're known for when it comes to handling a crisis. Do I make myself clear?"

Scott grins broadly and laughs.

"I won't be told what to do by my wife."

Sandra stands.

"Uh-huh—we'll see about that."

She slides her arms around his waist.

"Or you'll be sorry."

Scott grimaces and sighs.

"So says you."

Sandra tightens her grip around his waist. He notices and begins laughing. Sandra kisses him lightly. He smirks.

"I'll think about it. No promises. I lie a lot."

Sandra pulls Scott closer and whispers in his ear.

Page **90**

"That's cruel—even for you."

Sandra jabs Scott again and points at him with a determined look on her face. He turns to look at Justin.

20

"That's him. This is gonna be easier than I thought."

Brent pulls the car to a stop as Derek jumps out and runs toward Niels. Niels seems confused as he sees Derek coming toward him and tries to run but is grabbed seconds later.

"Who are you? Let me go."

Derek slaps Niels across the face as he continues to struggle. He begins dragging him toward where Brent is standing several yards away. Niels continues to struggle while Brent smiles broadly as Derek pushes him against the hood of the car.

"Let go of me this instant. My folks will have you arrested and jailed. I demand you let me go. Do you know who I am?"

Brent begins laughing loudly.

"Of course I know who you are. Why do you think I'm doing what I'm doing? If you know what's good for you, you'll keep your mouth shut—stop being such a frigging brat."

Niels rolls his eyes as he continues to struggle.

"I demand you let me go."

Brent looks at Derek.

"Didn't he just say that a second ago—this kid is really beginning to annoy me—too much mouth and not enough brains to back up his yammering. Maybe we should muzzle him."

Derek nods in agreement and hits Niels again. As he's hit across the face Niels reacts but seem unwilling to cry.

"What do you want? I demand an answer."

Brent makes a lewd gesture with his finger and grins.

"Isn't it obvious—money—lots of money."

Derek looks at Brent and they nod in agreement. Brent pulls out a roll of duct tape from under one of the car seats.

"You're gonna like this part of the deal—a kid like you needs to know his place—show respect to his elders."

Page 91

Niels watches while his hands are bound behind his back and his mouth covered with duct tape as he's shoved into the backseat of Brent's car. Niels seems terrified as both Brent and Derek begins laughing at him. He struggles as they point at him and laugh even louder. Derek walks toward the other side of the car as Brent make a lewd gesture at Niels and laughs again.

"Uh-huh—that's right Byron dear—you're gonna see how the real world works—see how money makes people do things they would never dare do unless they had no other choice."

Niels looks at Brent oddly and continues to struggle in the backseat as Brent gets into the car and begins driving away.

21

"Threats should never be made against a popular guy. A guy like me should be treated with the utmost respect."

Sandra watches as Scott sits down on a sofa near the entrance to the balcony inside their hotel room. He grins.

"Even Justin thought I was being threatened."

Sandra walks over to Scott.

"He said nothing of the sort—wouldn't dare."

She sits down next to Scott and grins.

"I'll expect you to behave yourself when we go to Los Angeles to meet with Wesley—no jealousy whatsoever."

Scott raises his hand.

"I'm not jealous. He's got nothing on me."

Sandra reaches out to tousle Scott's hair. She smirks slyly.

"He was quite the looker—seriously charming too."

Scott pulls Sandra toward him.

"I'll kick his ass."

Sandra gives Scott a warning look as he begins laughing. She strokes his cheek gently and kisses him lightly.

"This conversation is over."

Scott points his finger at Sandra and grins.

"I don't recall agreeing to such an arrangement."

Sandra playfully jabs Scott again.

Page 92

"Not one more word about Wesley Madison."

Scott watches as Sandra's hand slide down to the buttons on his Levi's. She gives him a cautious look and smiles.

"Maxwell isn't coming over for another hour. Seems to me you should be making use of the time—proving yourself."

Scott grins broadly and stands. He takes Sandra's hand and glances at the bedroom door. He begins to hum a tune.

22
Denmark Hill

Cliff taps his finger against the steering wheel of his car as he looks up toward a driveway several feet away. He turns to look at his cell phone lying in the seat next to him. He grins.

"That bitch is going to know me in ways she's never known a man before. I think it's time she and I find out what we have in common—what a guy like me can do for a miserable wretch like her. Lord knows she's not pretty—plain if truth be known. She looks like one of those girls from the 1950s—giving us guys a hard time—refusing to spread their legs and serve."

He clenches his fist angrily and turns to look at the driveway again. He grins as he sees Isabel walking toward a car parked under a large tree. He jumps out of his car suddenly.

TO BE CONTINUED

Page **93**

A Brief Look at the Fourth Episode

A planned kidnapping goes terribly awry where nothing is what it seems as several couples make complicated sexual matters even worse while a mentally disturbed individual begins to unravel.

Episode 4
Trouble in Progress

1
Blakely Mansion

"Niels is such a jerk—calling me names and still expecting me to go along with his plans to visit that deserted park."

Byron Blakely looks at this cell phone lying on a desk several feet away. He pauses and turns around. He shrugs.

"I hope he gets bitten—would serve him right."

He hears a sound and turns around to see Savannah Windsor standing in the doorway. She seems confused.

"Who were you talking to?"

Byron rolls his eyes and gestures.

"No one—I just saw Niels—he called me a chicken."

Savannah walks over to Byron.

"Why would he call you such a name? What happened between you two just now? Or do I even want to ask?"

Byron shrugs and walks over to the window. He turns around and sighs. He notices the look on Savannah's face.

"He wanted me to go with him to the park down the street—the one with the broken steps and hanging gate."

Savannah wags her finger at Byron and sighs.

"That park is no place for children. I heard there are drug dealers that hang around sometimes—selling drugs."

Byron begins to laugh at Savannah.

"No drug dealer would dare go into that park—place has spiders everywhere—not even a homeless person would want to go there and hang out—not unless they wanted to die with a bunch of spiders crawling all over them—*ugh*—no way."

Savannah clasps her hands together.

"Nevertheless I don't want you going into that park—if Niels wants to go—that's his deal—but not you—I forbid it."

Byron comes toward Savannah.

"You can't forbid me to do anything. If I want to go over there I can—no one tells me what to do. I can do as I please."

They share a glance. Savannah seems annoyed.

"How does your mother feel about the attitude you just took with me—does she feel the same way? Do tell."

Byron smirks and glances at his cell phone again.

"If you know what's good for you you'll watch what you say to me—one word and you're gonna be looking for a new job around this island—apartments are very expensive—is that what you want? Do you want to make an enemy out of me?"

Savannah looks at Byron oddly.

"I won't be blackmailed."

Byron takes a step closer to Savannah.

"How about we test that theory?"

They stare at each other for a few seconds.

2
Mandahl Bay Beach

Brent Crawford and Derek Ving step out of the car and turn to look at a rambling shack covered with vines and prickly flowers. Derek makes a gesture with his finger and gags.

"We're gonna be staying here?"

Brent looks back at the car and laughs.

Page **96**

"Should we stay at Frenchman's Reef instead? How about it? Should be book a room and stash the kid there? Well?"

Derek rolls his eyes and sighs loudly.

"OK—OK—I see your point. But I don't like it. This is not gonna be fun—especially with that spoiled rich brat."

Brent rolls his eyes knowingly and walks toward the car as Derek continues looking at the shack. Brent grins broadly.

"Uh-huh—Astrid will pay dearly for slighting me the way she did—that brat will net me millions—several in fact."

He begins laughing as he glances at Niels Anderssen lying in the backseat still bound with duct tape. He smirks slyly.

3
Creque Alley

"Ugh—the nerve of some people—you'd think given her circumstances she'd know better. She looks like a house."

Ava Fontaine makes a gagging gesture.

"The nerve of her—I was there when Cliff told Lindsay Ganz he wouldn't put a ring on her finger—told her to get an abortion—how shameful that she didn't take his advice—he even offered to pay for it—said he'd take her to the clinic too."

Greg Forbes watches as a pregnant teenage girl walks by where he and Ava are sitting. She stops and looks at Ava.

"Maybe before you talk trash about me behind my back you should look at your own sordid reputation. Of course to do that you'd have to get out from under whatever guy you're having sex with—how many has it been Ava—do you know?"

Ava reacts to the slight and stands up.

"How dare you speak to me like that especially given your circumstances with Cliff—you got played—admit it."

Lindsay takes a step closer to Ava.

"I heard you made a surprise visit to the free clinic the other day—oh, I wonder why—could it be you caught something from that vile Omar Cortez last week—not that it would surprise anyone who knows what a raging slut you've been lately."

Ava seems about to slap Lindsay but suddenly takes a step back and glances at Greg. Lindsay grins and heads toward the front door of the small diner. Ava angrily clenches her fist.

"Did you actually make a trip to the free clinic last week?"

Ava turns to look at Greg. Her eyes seem on fire as she sits down again. He leans across the table and sighs loudly.

"Well? Did you? I think I have a right to know given our recent sexual history together—certainly wouldn't want to catch anything—especially from someone like Omar Cortez—that guy has a reputation ten times worse than mine—beds anything."

Ava makes a lewd gesture with her finger.

4

Byron is swimming laps as he notices his mother coming toward him with a cell phone in her hand. Astrid Blakely seems somewhat upset and motions for him to stop swimming.

"Have you talked with Niels recently?"

Byron shakes his head and shrugs.

"Not since this morning when he called me a chicken. I told him where to go—haven't heard from him since."

Astrid looks at her cell phone.

"His mother just called and seems worried. Said she hasn't seen him in hours. She thought maybe you might know?"

Byron climbs out of the pool.

"Niels is a jerk. I don't care if I ever see him again."

Astrid seems shocked by Byron's comment. As he walks by her she grabs his arm. They look at each other for a second.

"I don't like your tone of voice young man."

Byron rolls his eyes.

"It's the way I feel. Why should I pretend?"

He jerks free and heads into the house. She turns to look at the pool again and sighs. The cell phone begins buzzing.

"Where is that child?"

She sighs and answers the phone and shrugs.

"Byron said he hasn't seen him for several hours."

Page **98**

She walks toward the edge of the patio and looks toward the thick grove of trees in a distance. She shakes her head.

"Uh-huh—I agree. Maybe it's time you call the police and report him missing—you can never be too careful these days."

She nods several times in agreement and sighs.

5
Denmark Hill

"You have exactly one minute to leave me alone or I'll call the cops and have you arrested. I'll lie if I have to."

Cliff Nickerson looks at Isabel Black and then at the street nearby. He shakes his fist at her. She gestures at him.

"You and I will never be a "thing"—you disgust me—vile disgusting creature. I'd rather have sex with a dirty, smelly troll that lives under a bridge—anyone but you—*ugh*—gross."

Cliff watches as she pulls out her cell phone.

"You're gonna regret insulting me, *bitch*—that I promise you—no one gets away with calling me names—slighting me like I'm some lowly dork—we're gonna dance—that I promise."

He gets into his car and drives away.

"*Ugh*—he really needs to get a reality check."

She faces her car again and sighs.

6

"What happens when we get the money from your ex? Are you still on board with what we planned? Take the brat out and dump him at sea—let him fight it out with hungry sharks?"

Brent gives Derek a knowing look.

"What do you think?"

At the corner of the shack Niels seems in shock as he listens to what he's hearing. They notice and both begin laughing. Derek walks over to where Niels is sitting, tied to a chair. He grins broadly as he begins kicking him gleefully. He laughs loudly.

"We're gonna kill you Byron—painfully—slowly."

He turns to Brent and begins laughing hysterically.

"He'll never see his momma again."

Niels reacts again as they point at him and laugh. He seems panicked as he looks at the duct tape binding his hands.

7
Hoya Coffee Corporate Offices
Puerto Rico

"Did she say why? Give a reason why she was selling her plantation? Something must have triggered it—money?"

Gavin Ayers shakes his head and sighs.

"Not a word—just said she was selling her plantation in South Africa—getting out of the coffee business entirely."

Milo Wiley walks toward the window and looks out at the city below. He seems upset as he clenches his fists. He shrugs.

"Tabletop Plantation grows one of the best coffees we offer—gotta make a deal to secure it before she sells."

He faces Gavin again and gestures.

"Get her assistant on the phone. Tell him we're prepared to offer twice whatever Madame Valois is being offered."

Gavin nods in agreement as he picks up his cell phone and begins dialing. At that moment Alexander de Hoya comes into the office with a strange look on his face. He stops suddenly.

"I have to go to St. Thomas for a few days."

Milo seems confused.

"The Tabletop deal is in crisis mode—I need your help to make sure Madame Valois doesn't give us the shaft."

Alexander rolls his eyes.

"Can't you handle it Milo? Alexis is in one of his moods again—got to make good with him—before it's too late."

Milo waves his hand in the air.

"Go—see if I care. Let Alexis play ping pong with your emotions until you wise up and see the light—face reality."

Alexander glances at Milo and Gavin.

"I'll call Madame Valois later and charm her."

Page **100**

He sighs loudly and leaves without saying another word. As the door slams behind him Gavin turns to face Milo.

"He was quite close to her a few years back—shared her bed plenty if I recall—charmed her silly—kept her happy."

Milo shoots Gavin a nasty look.

"That was then—this is now. Catching him in bed with her daughter soured her feelings for him—took it quite badly."

Gavin looks at his cell phone again.

"I read somewhere that her daughter once dated the son of **Princess Stephanie**. It must have been quite the come down to end up in bed with Alexander—from royalty to nobody."

Milo seems irritated by the comment.

"How about you stick to your job and leave the low rent *Entertainment Tonight* material for the supermarket tabloids."

Gavin nods and begins dialing as Milo nervously wrings his hands several times. Seconds later the phone is picked up.

8
Neltjeberg Bay Beach

"This place is beautiful—like right out of romance novel or something. The waves are so quiet and serene—so perfect."

John Smythe grins and gestures with his hand.

"I told you I know all sorts of places around this island. I was told about it last year by one of the locals while I was at the supermarket. Said the road was a nightmare but the beach was worth the hassle—he wasn't wrong. Place has become popular with tourists lately from what I heard—word of mouth."

He kicks his bare feet at the sand.

"There's an old plantation somewhere near here—place is overgrown—but you can still see the walls—hear voices."

Shirley Lindstrom grimaces and sighs.

"Don't you think about it John Smythe. We're not going by that plantation—ghost hunting or otherwise—no way."

John pulls Shirley toward him and laughs.

"It might be fun—like being in an old movie?"

Page **101**

Shirley jabs John in the chest. He winces in pain.

"I was only suggesting we could do it? Seeing if there was interest on your part—wondering if maybe you were game."

Shirley jabs John again and grins.

"Nice try—but no way will I go anywhere near those ruins. I heard too many tales by the locals about ghosts—some of the stories are probably made up for entertaining tourists—but not all—the history of the Caribbean is drenched with blood."

John rolls his eyes and gestures playfully.

"Says who? I don't play the ghost game. People can say whatever they want—tell tales. There's no proof either way."

Shirley shoots John a cautious look.

"I'm still not going with you into the jungle."

John turns to face the ocean again. He looks across the channel toward Inner Brass Island and grins broadly.

"You and I are going to pay that island a visit soon—count on it—perfect place for a picnic—got to rent a sailboat."

Shirley looks at John curiously.

"Do you know how to sail?"

John wraps his arms around Shirley.

"Uh-huh—lots of things about me you don't know. Like for instance Shirley, I'm really good at charming my girlfriend."

She jabs him playfully and laughs.

"Says who?"

John kisses Shirley.

"Says me—your charming boyfriend."

He looks out at the island again.

"You and I have a date with that island next week. No use pretending I'm not a cool guy—I'm the best you'll ever get."

Shirley pushes John away and grins.

"You seem pretty sure of yourself John—what about what I think? Does it matter? What if I think differently? Well?"

John grins and pulls Shirley toward him.

"You like me—I know it and so do you—end of story."

He pulls Shirley closer and winks at her.

"I think you should marry me—make it legal."

Shirley seems in shock and gasps.

"I accept."

John begins laughing.

"Just like that—no hesitation?"

Shirley wags her finger at John and sighs.

"Don't you try to wiggle out now—I accept your proposal of marriage—there's no way out—I won't change my mind."

John laughs once more and gestures.

"I wouldn't think of backing out—I said it and I meant it—I want you to be my wife—make a bunch of babies with me."

Shirley wags her finger at John.

"I'm not big on morning sickness."

John looks out toward the ocean again and grins.

"Let's just see if I can impregnate you first."

Shirley tousles John's hair.

9
Mandahl Bay Beach

"What do you mean I don't have the right kid? I got the brat right here—he's tied up at the moment—can't talk."

Brent runs his fingers through his hair.

"Oh fuck—damn it—are you serious Savannah—you're on the level with me about Byron Blakely? But I grabbed him right outside Astrid's house. How was I supposed to know?"

He stops and looks at the shack.

"What did they say? Did his parents call the cops? Did they send out a search party for their wretched pre-teen spawn?"

He runs his fingers through his hair.

"Of course I know how this looks. That miserable brat got lucky—and the one I have has been a handful. Kid is seriously more trouble than he's worth—and now this bit of bad news."

He stops and looks at the shack again.

"OK—call me back as soon as you know what the deal is concerning his parents—what they are gonna do—clue me."

He sighs and hastily shuts off his cell phone.

Page 103

"One brat over the other—I don't care much either way if truth be known—Niels Anderssen will work just fine actually."

He begins laughing as he looks at the ocean raging below the jagged cliffs where the shack is perched among weeds.

"That bratty rich kid better play ball with us—or he'll find that an accidental fall from a cliff will result in certain death."

He dances a jig and smirks. He hums a tune.

"It would be too bad if he tried to get away after his parents paid for his safe return and he ended up falling into the ocean below courtesy of help from Derek and yours truly."

Brent snaps his fingers several times.

"If the kid were to die then he couldn't finger either of us later—couldn't give details—a dead brat is better than a live one when it comes to making sure there are no loose ends."

He reaches the shack and turns around.

"Got to convince Derek to go this route—as far as I'm concerned money is money—doesn't matter how we get it."

Brent reaches out to grab the doorknob.

10
Main Street

"I already told you the answer was no. I don't dig nature walks—especially if it involves creepy old plantations."

Boris Birney rolls his eyes as he looks at John walking across a pristine-looking beach. He shakes his fist at John.

"The answer is no—don't ask me again."

Boris turns to face Alison Gluck as he shuts off his cell phone. He seems annoyed as he clenches his fist several times.

"He never gives up—one disaster after another."

Alison stops and faces Boris.

"Why don't you go with John? How bad could it be?"

Boris gives Alison a knowing look.

"I don't dig creepy ruins of old abandoned plantations in the middle of a vermin-infested jungle—don't want to see weird things that shouldn't actually be there either—like no way."

He runs his fingers through his hair.

"I'm a city-bred boy—never been camping and I've never missed not being one with nature—he's on his own this time."

He notices his cell phone buzzing again.

11
Estate Mafolie

"I don't know where he is right now. He's probably with his girlfriend—hanging out at some deserted beach or other."

Ingrid de Hoya seems annoyed as she looks at the reaction of her ex-husband. She watches as Alexander runs his fingers through his hair. He sighs loudly several times before he faces her again. She turns to look at Jordan McKinney who is standing in the doorway leading to a marble-tiled balcony. He shrugs.

"He's partial to Stumpy Bay Beach."

Alexander turns to look at Ingrid. He winces.

"Isn't that beach virtually impossible to get to without a boat? From what I remember the road is badly washed out."

Ingrid gives Alexander a knowing look.

"Alexis apparently doesn't care."

Alexander looks at his cell phone again.

"He hasn't replied to my text yet?"

Ingrid stands and gestures.

"Now you know how I feel every day."

Alexander looks at his cell phone again and sighs.

"What about this girl? Who is she?"

Ingrid shoots Jordan a look.

"Marisa Rossmore."

Alexander seems confused.

"Is she rich?"

Ingrid rolls her eyes.

"I didn't ask. I assume given what she was wearing the day I met her. Rest assured she doesn't shop at Kmart."

Alexander walks toward the balcony and stops.

"Should I conclude he's sleeping with her?"

Ingrid seems upset and faces Alexander directly.

"Why don't you ask him and see where that gets you? I'm sure he'll tell you the truth—the same way you did when he asked if you were playing house with the hired help—how about it?"

Alexander glances at Jordan, who looks away.

"One thing doesn't have anything to do with the other."

Ingrid seems enraged as she looks at Alexander.

"How would you know? Did you ask him?"

Alexander seems stung by her words.

12
Blakely Driveway

"Why would anyone want to kidnap Niels? We're not a wealthy family—we got some money—but not nearly enough."

Astrid shakes her head and faces Valerie Anderssen as the woman seems about to lose her mind. In a distance she sees Savannah talking with Byron. She faces Valerie once more.

"They're gonna find him—this island isn't that big. There's only so many places to hide—he'll turn up really soon."

Valerie nods in agreement as she wipes a tear from her eye and she notices several police officers patrolling the area in front of her home. She wipes another tear from her eye.

"Maybe they thought he was someone else?"

Astrid seems confused and sighs.

"There aren't many children that live on this block. Most of the people are older—hardly any families to speak of."

Valerie looks back at Byron and Savannah.

"What about Byron?"

Astrid glances at Byron and then back at Valerie.

"What about him?"

"What if someone thought Niels was Byron? Grabbed him as he walked along the road—thinking he was Byron."

Astrid seems frightened and turns to look at where Byron and Savannah are standing. Valerie notices her reaction.

13
Mafolie Hotel

"Oh-oh—here we go again—CNN has latched onto a story about some child's kidnapping—turning it into major news."

Scott Malone leans back on the sofa as he glances over at Sandra King sitting in front of a laptop computer. He sighs.

"Some kid just up and vanished apparently—the local cops are looking under every rock on this island—rich people."

Sandra wags her finger at Scott.

"You don't know if the family is rich."

"I highly doubt they'd make this much effort if the kid was some latchkey brat without influence. Uh-huh—he's rich."

His cell phone begins buzzing. He grimaces.

"Roland is calling—what a surprise."

Sandra watches as Scott begins talking to Roland. He seems annoyed as he walks toward the balcony and shrugs.

14
Havensight Mall

Silas Bell looks back at the covered parking lot as he walks toward his car. He grins broadly as he glances at the bag in his hand and smirks. A few people walk past him in a hurried rush.

"I wonder what my dear brother will do when he finds himself at the other end of my gun—will he plead for his life?"

He grins as he reaches his rental car.

"Once he and his offspring are out of the way it'll be mine—all mine. No longer will I have to beg for scraps."

He throws the bag into the car and laughs.

15
Frenchman's Reef Resort

"Oh my God—it's you. Oh, I can't believe I'm actually meeting you. I watched everything on CNN—saw the rescue."

Page **107**

Victoria de Hoya smiles as she looks at a woman standing inches away from her table. Marla Jefferson excitedly extends her hand as Victoria notices the young man with her. He couldn't be more than twenty. Marla seems in awe as she sighs loudly.

"It was like something out of the movies. I can't believe you and the others made it out alive—it was incredible."

Victoria seems uneasy but continues smiling.

"It all happened so fast that most of it is a blur now. My daughter and I didn't know we were being filmed until later."

Marla shakes her head several times.

"Are you going to be at the book signing tomorrow?"

Victoria nods as she eyes the young man again.

"I'll be there—for a photo shoot."

Marla nods again.

"I flew all the way from New England to be able to meet Sandra King in person. It was nice meeting you today. Well, enjoy your dinner—much appreciated. I hope I didn't disturb you?"

Victoria gestures with her hand and smiles.

"Maybe I'll see you at the signing."

Marla nods again and leads Greg Sharpe away. Victoria watches them walk toward a table at the other end of the restaurant and sighs loudly. Her eyes seem glued to Greg.

"What a choice piece of male wonder. No doubt he knows his way around the bedroom. His workouts must be intense."

She licks her lips several times.

"I could use someone like him in my bed."

She seductively licks her lips again and sighs loudly.

"I wonder if he has a brother."

She watches as Marla and Greg share an intimate kiss. As they kiss Victoria turns to look around at the small restaurant.

"It's time I take my life into my own hands again—stop waiting for someone to make themselves known—got to go hunting if I want to stop sleeping alone—enough is enough."

She reaches for her cell phone and smirks.

"It's time Maxwell Pendergraft and I got reacquainted. He certainly wouldn't be a disappointment—not even a little."

She sighs as she hears his voice.

"How would you like to join me for dinner?"

She smiles broadly as she watches Maxwell Pendergraft nod in agreement from the balcony of his hotel room.

"I can be there in twenty minutes."

Victoria seems pleased.

16
Nickerson Driveway

"What are you doing here Lindsay? I thought I told you we were through? Made it clear I was done with you—over."

Lindsay glares at Cliff as he seems reluctant to look at her stomach. She edges closer toward him as he backs away.

"This is your child Cliff—yours and mine."

Cliff runs his fingers through his hair.

"How do I know it's mine? You're a frigging slut—fucked plenty of other guys—played around endlessly—used me."

Lindsay slaps Cliff across the face.

"How dare you speak to me like that? It's yours and you know it—you took a DNA test—or did you forget about that."

Cliff makes a lewd gesture with his finger.

"Those things can be faked."

Lindsay seems ready to slap Cliff again as he backs away from her. He turns to look toward his house. She sighs.

"I'm due in less than a month—there's no way you can deny what's going to happen—fatherhood is pending."

Cliff runs his fingers through his hair again.

"I already told you I'm not the father—end of story."

Lindsay angrily grabs Cliff by the arm.

"I don't care what you say—you're the father and once this baby arrives you'll step up to the plate and take responsibility."

Cliff begins laughing.

"Or what—you'll have me killed?"

Lindsay shoots Cliff a warning look and grins.

"This island is surrounded by water."

Page 109

Cliff seems confused by the comment.

"What's that supposed to mean? Are you threatening my life Lindsay? Giving me an ultimatum? Well, spill already."

Lindsay looks at her stomach.

"It would be such a shame if our unborn child never got to know you—cemeteries are so impersonal—unfriendly."

Cliff reacts as Lindsay turns away.

17

Water Island

"I don't know—Ava hates me—she said so as much when she saw me with Lance Striker last week. Demanded I leave him alone after she caught me giving him a quickie blowjob. Said she wouldn't warn me again—said she'd tell my boyfriend."

Greg smirks as he faces Whitney Wilkins.

"Ava Fontaine doesn't own me. She and I are just friends with benefits and nothing more. She knows how I roll."

Whitney pulls Greg toward her.

"You bad boys are all the same—you'll say anything to score with us—fucking girls and receiving blowjobs are all you care about—no shame whatsoever—my mother was right."

Greg grins broadly and laughs.

"Uh-huh—got a problem with how we think?"

Whitney lets her finger slide across Greg's bulging erection under his faded Levi's. He grins slyly as he watches her begin to play with the zipper. He glances at the door.

"Maybe you should lock the bedroom door in case your mother comes home and catches us in the act. One time was enough if you recall—your mother warned me—threatened."

Whitney licks her lips and grins.

"Since when do you respond to threats?"

Greg glances at the bed and then at the door.

"It's up to you—either way I intend to fuck you. Enjoy a piece before I head back to the ferry leaving for Crown Bay."

Whitney strokes Greg's erection.

Page **110**

"Don't you care a little bit for me? Do I mean anything to you other than a good time? Do you respect me as a person?"

Greg begins laughing and gestures.

"What is this? Have you been watching one of those stupid talk shows where women complain that they're treated like a piece of meat by every dude they sleep with? Ugh."

He points his finger at Whitney.

"Give me a break already."

She seems upset and turns away.

18
Anderssen Estate

Astrid watches as a police car pulls out of the driveway and seems upset. She runs her fingers through her hair.

"Do the police know anything yet? Have anyone called? Asking for something? Have there been any contact at all?"

Valerie looks at Astrid and sighs.

"Nothing—no calls whatsoever—none of the neighbors saw anything. It's all playing out like a bad dream—terrible."

Astrid puts her arms around Valerie.

"Have you told Viktor?"

Valerie shakes her head several times.

"He's on his way back from Virgin Gorda. Cut his business meeting short—freaked out with worry—asking questions."

Valerie glances at the front door.

"I still can't believe this is really happening. Niels isn't the type that would get into a stranger's car. He wouldn't fall prey to something like that—someone must have taken him by force earlier—probably had help—Niels is a feisty kid—aggressive."

Astrid gives Valerie a knowing look.

"This island isn't that big. Earlier I heard one of the police officers say that they were bringing in the FBI tomorrow."

Valerie reacts and faces Astrid.

"Do you think whoever took Niels is one of those child predator killers that seeks out young boys—rapes them."

Astrid seems unable to answer and shrugs.

"I don't think this is one of those cases. Like you said earlier, I think it was Byron they were after. Byron's father was one of the richest men in the world—plenty of enemies."

She runs her fingers through her hair again.

"Whoever took Niels won't be able to leave the island. The airport is being watched as is every dock. There's no way anyone can leave without being seen. It's just a matter of time before they get caught—and then everything will make sense."

Valerie wipes a tear from her eye and nods.

19

"You haven't changed one bit—still gorgeous as ever—a welcomed sight for sore eyes—how have you been Victoria?"

Victoria grins broadly as she ushers Maxwell into her hotel room and closes the door. She glances at his tight Levi's.

"Still nice on the eyes—it's a sin you're so hot."

Maxwell smirks and pulls Victoria toward him. They kiss for a few seconds. Victoria fumbles with his belt buckle.

"I think we should play a bit before we have dinner. Enjoy a moment together. Pick up where we left off two years ago."

Maxwell laughs and lets Victoria lead him down the hallway toward an open door. She stops at the door.

"It's been a while since I had someone in my life that treated me the way you did—left an impression that day."

Maxwell watches as Victoria closes the door behind them and faces him again. She tugs at his belt buckle and smirks.

"Have you been lonely for female company?"

Maxwell wags his finger at Victoria.

"I'm a single guy—with lots of girlfriends."

Victoria jabs Maxwell in the chest and grins.

"Is that your way of saying you've been in plenty of beds since we last met? Thoroughly enjoyed the company of beautiful women you've charmed silly—had your way with them?"

Maxwell makes a lewd gesture with his finger.

"I think I'll take the fifth."

Victoria slides her hand into Maxwell's boxer briefs and looks at him. He laughs as her finger dances across his swelling erection. She pushes him down on the bed and sighs.

<hr>

The Next Day

<hr>

20

Main Street

"Roland is insisting on a story about that missing kid. Says he won't back down—demands I follow through—ordered."

Sandra jabs Scott as they walk down the street past several stores. She seems annoyed and sighs loudly.

"That man always seems to know how to ruin a perfect vacation—I'm beginning to think he has a bug on you."

She jabs him again and grins.

"Your phone would be my guess."

Scott grins broadly.

"Uh-huh—and last night you told me you thought Roland might have had a microchip implanted into me when I had my tonsils removed last year. Demanded I strip so you could check personally—left nothing to chance—explored for hours."

Sandra pulls Scott closer and laughs.

"I don't regret one moment of what happened last night. You had it coming for looking so cute—besides, a wife has the right to enjoy her husband's body—sample his wares."

Scott wags his finger at her.

"Uh-huh—I slept like a baby afterwards in case you were wondering—so tired—tired but with a huge grin on my face."

Sandra reaches out to kiss Scott.

"Justin expects me at Havensight Mall in an hour. The signing starts at eleven. I expect you to be there—smiling."

Scott gives Sandra a knowing look.

"Of course I'll be there. Wouldn't want to miss all those adoring fans—telling me how cute I am—uh-huh—yeah."

Sandra jabs Scott in the chest yet again.

"Don't you dare upstage me—taking all the attention for yourself—you're just there for support—and nothing more."

Scott gestures with his hand and laughs.

"I make no such promises. I'm gonna be myself."

Sandra shoots Scott a warning look.

21
Mandahl Bay Beach

"They're gonna find you—that boy's parents are leaving no stone unturned. They've brought in the FBI for help."

Savannah nervously watches for a reaction from Brent Crawford but sees none. He glances back at the shack.

"That kid has been a holy terror. Frigging brat is mouthy and doesn't shut up for a second. I've had to keep him tied up with duct tape. I swear I'd like nothing more than to wring his fucking neck just to watch him die. Damn kid thinks he knows everything—told us he's gonna blab once the cops catch us."

Savannah seems nervous and sighs.

"You can't kill him Brent—they'll fry you for sure if this thing goes south. Murdering a child will result in the public going crazy until someone pays for it. Just ask for a ransom and then get the hell away from St. Thomas—leave everything behind."

Brent looks at Savannah curiously.

"Have you forgotten you're involved in this mess up to your eyeballs? Whatever happens to me and Derek also happens to you—that brat will finger us all—send us all up the river."

He points toward the shack and grimaces.

"A fall from the cliff will certainly kill that boy—and with him out of the way there'll be no one that can indentify us."

An evil grin spreads across Brent's face.

"Of course such an accident will only happen after we get his parents to hand over a pile of cash—millions in fact."

He watches Savannah's reaction and laughs as he notices Derek standing outside the shack. Brent turns around.

"He's almost at wit's end over this situation—would love nothing better than to pitch that brat off the cliff and watch him fall to his death—laughing joyously as the kid screams."

Savannah grabs Brent's arm.

"We had it all planned out—you were supposed to wait until I brought Byron here—you weren't supposed to be outside his house—what if Astrid had seen you? What then?"

Brent runs his fingers through his hair.

"I lost my head—thought I'd drive by and see the area for myself—know where the side streets were—and then I saw *him* walking along the road acting like he owned the world."

He clenches his fist angrily.

"Grabbing that spoiled rich brat seemed so easy we just decided to do it—shut him immediately with duct tape."

He grabs Savannah's arm and shakes her.

"That kid isn't going to ruin my plans—I'll kill him first. Do you hear me—he's better off dead at the bottom of a cliff."

He glances back at the shack and faces Savannah again. He lets go of her arm and sighs loudly. She grimaces.

"I'm going back—Astrid will get suspicious if I'm gone too long—said I was going to get my nails done in town."

Brent looks at Savannah curiously.

"I hate that damn bitch for how she treated me. She threw me out like trash and never thought twice about it as she went looking for better prospects right afterwards. Uh-huh—I ought to take out that dude she likes so much—kill the bastard."

A look of concern comes over Savannah's face as she watches Brent. He seems to be entertaining the idea of killing yet another person. She nervously points her finger at him.

"The last thing you need is more trouble. Stay away from Peter Zimmerman—the less drama you create the better."

Brent flies into a rage and grabs Savannah's arm again and spins her around. His face contorts into an evil grimace.

"Don't you dare tell me what to do—this is my show and I'm gonna do whatever the hell I feel like doing—and if I want to rub out that frigging loser then I'll do it—probably with a gun."

Page 115

He begins laughing as he lets go of her. Savannah turns to look at her car and sighs. She seems worried. He smiles.

"I think I'm gonna do it right after I pitch that brat over the cliff—once his stupid parents hand over a wad of cash."

He makes a slashing gesture with his hand.

"Zimmerman is next on my list once the rotten kid is lying face down on the rocks with endless broken bones. With the kid out of the way I'll shoot her beloved at close range to insure that bastard doesn't have an open casket—make Astrid freak."

Savannah opens the door to her sedan. Brent looks at the shack again and watches as she starts the engine of the car.

22
Reynolds Estate

Armand Bell watches as several security guards begin patrolling the grounds before he drives toward the gates.

"That creep Silas better stay clear of my family if he knows what's good for him. He should have stayed in Australia."

He drives along a tree-lined street heading down the hill toward the city of Charlotte Amalie. He glances at his watch nervously as he looks back several times. Armand seems uneasy, almost as if he expects someone to be following him. He pulls out a cell phone and begins dialing while he continues driving.

23
Frenchman's Reef Resort

"If your father knew I paid for your trip to the islands he'd have a massive coronary. Your father would certainly lose it if he found out his son had taken his girlfriend away from him."

Marla shoots Greg a sly look as she pushes him against the hood of her rental car. She kisses him passionately.

"But the truth is when I met you I couldn't stop thinking of what could be—then you made your move by the pool."

Greg laughs as he kisses Marla.

"I told you my father was good but I was twice as good. Told you how hard I was at the moment—rigid and ready."

Marla looks down at Greg's bulging erection under his Lycra shorts. She reaches out to stroke it as he grins broadly.

"We had sex in your car ten minutes later. I couldn't say no to such a handsome young man—you wanted me so badly."

Greg kisses Marla passionately again.

"He has no idea I'd been screwing you for the past week and a half—thinks I had a horny girlfriend—marveled at the pack of condoms he found in the trash—asked how many times I was fucking her—warned me she might try to play me for a fool."

He begins laughing gleefully.

"If he only knew I was fucking *his* girlfriend."

Marla wags her finger at Greg.

"I never told him I was his girlfriend—if he assumed then that was his doing—we're friendly—nothing more."

Greg gives Marla a knowing look.

"Uh-huh—you led him astray without a doubt. The same way you teased me the day we met—dared me to act."

Marla strokes Greg's cheek with her finger.

"I'm not going to admit to anything. Besides we're both consenting adults—you're a college guy at Emerson and I'm on the board at your school—in an alternative universe you could be my son—dating my beloved daughter is she was still alive."

Greg seems uneasy and turns away.

"I'm sorry about what happened to your daughter. Sorry that I never got to know her. I bet she was really nice."

Marla slowly wipes a tear from her eye and sighs. She faces the hotel briefly and reaches out to hug Greg warmly.

"She was—best daughter a mother could ask for—I still miss her even after all these years. I visit her grave every chance I get. But it's just so hard sometimes—with people talking trash about me all the time. I'm thinking of moving to Portland. It's not too far from Boston where you and your father live. My ex has moved on too—begun dating a local girl from what he said."

Greg pulls Marla toward him and grins.

Page **117**

"How about we go to that book signing—and afterwards head over to one of those deserted beaches we saw online. Find a shady place under a huge coconut tree and make love."

Marla looks down at Greg's erection and sighs loudly.

"I don't know what I did to deserve such a nice young man like you but I'm grateful—you've brought me to incredible places I could only have imagined before—a point of no return."

Greg smirks as he opens the car door.

24
Bordeaux Road

"No way will I do such a thing. What kind of guy do you think I am? Go find yourself another chump to play."

Omar Cortez runs his fingers through his hair as he leans against his car and watches Ava's reaction cautiously.

"She has it coming—that whore will ruin Cliff Nickerson's life once she gives birth to his baby. She made it quite clear with her behavior. She wants him for herself—wants him to marry her and settle down—ugh—how horrible. She's certifiable."

Omar gestures with his hand.

"Not my problem—Cliff knew better than to tangle with a girl like that—every guy in town avoided her like the plague knowing her deal—but Cliff decided to play with a loaded gun and ended up getting caught in her witchy web. Good riddance."

Ava comes closer to Omar and smiles.

"It would truly be a shame if Stanley Strauss found out you seduced his wild fourteen-year-old daughter and filmed what happened in the backseat of your car. I heard he has a really sharp machete in his garage—heard he hates you by the way."

She licks her lips several times.

"I know I promised to keep what you did with his daughter between us—but oh—I'm not sure I'll be able keep our agreement if you decide not to help me get Cliff Nickerson off the hook with that horrible troll Lindsay Ganz. Then again Strauss has a right to know his daughter was soiled by a promiscuous college guy."

Page 118

She licks her lips again and reaches out to touch Omar's lips as he reacts to her threat. She leans closer and whispers.

"Don't push me Cortez—I'll tell. You know I always do what I say—and Stanley Strauss is going to be told if you don't help Cliff get rid of his unborn child. The only question left is whether you'll play—or risk being chopped into tiny pieces."

She begins giggling as she sees his reaction. She turns to look at the deserted road again. She points to his car.

"That reminds me—my cousin would really hate to find out you slept with his girlfriend last summer—fucked her in his apartment of all places—didn't even bother to use a condom."

She reaches for her cell phone and grimaces.

"How about I tell him right now?"

Omar looks at Ava and sighs. She grins.

25
Havensight Mall

Lines of people can be seen standing in front of a boutique bookstore as several large vans with cameras show up. People continue milling about as they watch the news crew begin setting up large video cameras and satellite dishes. In a parking lot nearby among a throng of people Maxwell and Victoria are seen walking toward the bookstore. In a distance Sandra and Scott arrive and watch as Justin Manslow walks over to greet them.

TO BE CONTINUED

A Brief Look at the Fifth Episode

A book signing reaps more than sales for those in attendance as a blackmail threat leads to someone's death while a kidnapped boy witnesses a strange event that has meaning for someone else.

Episode 5
Once Backwards

1
Bordeaux Road

Omar Cortez seems somewhat confused as he looks at the body lying at his feet with a broken neck. He shrugs as he looks at Ava Fontaine again. He wrings his hand several times.

"She gave me no choice."

He looks at the deserted road and grimaces.

"Got to ditch her before someone happens along and sees my handiwork—and fingers me. Damn blackmailing bitch."

He looks around again and casually pushes Ava's body under some shrubs near a trail leading toward a nearby beach.

"Got to play it cool for a couple of hours until they find the body—then act shocked—act like I had no knowledge."

He grins broadly as he walks toward his car.

"No one blackmails me and gets away with it—especially not Ava. Her reputation speaks for itself—skank queen."

He grabs his cell phone and stops suddenly.

"Maybe I'll spread a rumor that Cliff Nickerson took her out—hint that Ava Fontaine was blackmailing him for weeks."

He grins and gets into his car. He looks at Ava's car parked several feet away before he drives away. He sighs loudly.

"At least Lindsay Ganz won't have to worry about Ava spreading vicious lies about her anymore—good riddance."

Omar begins to laugh as he heads back toward town.

2
Reynolds Estate

"Damn him. Frigging bastard has the place swarming with security—but no matter—I'm gonna take him out regardless."

Silas Bell glances at the gun lying on the passenger seat beside him. He looks back once as he drives down the street.

"He's a dead man—a frigging dead man."

He clenches his fists angrily.

"I think it's time I pay his kid a visit."

He begins laughing as he looks at the gun again.

3
Blakely Mansion

"I don't see why I can't go outside today. What's the big deal? I'm sick of staying in my room—there's nothing to do."

Byron Blakely stands in front of Savannah Windsor with a cold stare as she ignores him. He glances at the door and sighs.

"Seriously, you can't keep me in here all day."

Savannah looks at the key in her hand.

"I can and I will."

She watches as his eyes wander toward the balcony.

"Don't even think about it."

Byron rolls his eyes at her and shrugs.

"I'm gonna tell my mother to fire you."

Savannah points her finger at him and grins.

"Who do you think told me to keep you here? Go ahead and waste your time—you've got no say in the matter."

Byron seems upset and looks at the balcony again.

"I bet I can climb down the wall like *Spider-Man*. Get away from you and my mother. If **Tom Holland** can do it—so can I."

Savannah laughs and waves her hand.

"Go ahead—try it if you like. But remember one thing before you do—you're not an actor—and there are no special effects to help you if you fall from the balcony—you'll die."

Byron shakes his fist at Savannah.

"You're no fun at all."

Savannah wags her finger at Byron and smirks.

"Tell it to someone who cares young man."

She watches as he looks toward the balcony again.

4

Forbes Driveway

"Where the fuck is she?"

Greg Forbes shuts off his cell phone and faces his brother. He seems upset as he runs his fingers through his hair.

"Just forget her already—like I told you earlier when you called—she's probably in the backseat of someone's car. I'll bet you anything she's under Cliff Nickerson as we speak. She has a thing for him despite what she says. They shacked up plenty."

Bryce Forbes makes a lewd gesture with his finger as he sees his brother's shocked reaction. He walks over to Greg.

"Ava Fontaine isn't worth it—every guy has had a piece of her in the last six plus months—including yours truly."

He grins as he jabs his brother.

"I know she told you we hardly knew each other. But she lied. We know each other really well—biblically in fact."

He laughs as Greg reacts to his comment.

"Let it go already little bro—Ava Fontaine's not into you. You were just someone to make Cliff jealous. Why do you think she hates Lindsay Ganz so much? Lindsay stands in Ava's way of having Cliff for herself. Sooner or later he'll have to fall in line and play the daddy role. Lindsay knows it and so does Ava."

Greg runs his fingers through his hair again.

Page **123**

"I'm not in love with Ava—I know exactly what kind of girl she is—I'm just concerned that's all. She threatened Lindsay."
Bryce shoots Greg a curious look.
"Does Lindsay know?"
Greg shakes his head and sighs.
"I don't think so."
He looks at his cell phone.
"I didn't think Ava was serious. She and Lindsay got into it over Cliff yesterday. Lindsay bested her and Ava took it badly."
At that moment Greg's cell phone begins ringing.

5
Havensight Mall

"Who knew you were this popular? There's not even one copy left. I'd say we have a bestseller on our hands no doubt."
Sandra King turns to face Justin Manslow as he glances at the empty table nearby. She seems pleased and nods several times. As Justin talks, her eyes wander over to where Scott Malone is standing. He seems engrossed in a conversation with a woman Sandra doesn't recognize. Justin notices and grins.
"I see your hubby is quite the magnet."
Sandra shoots Justin a harsh look.
"Who is she?"
Justin shrugs.
"No idea."
Sandra seems upset as she watches Scott laughing and seeming to enjoy the company of the unknown woman.

6
Mandahl Bay Beach

"They'll catch and hang both of you for kidnapping me. I'll testify—tell them everything I know. You're *so* dead."
Brent Crawford seems a bit annoyed as Niels Anderssen continues to talk—seemingly aware of their situation.

"You won't say a word to anyone—not one word will ever be heard from your mouth—dead children tell no tales."

Niels Anderssen rolls his eyes.

"Uh-huh—I'll tell when they catch you. Neither of you know what you're up against. My dad is no one to mess with."

Brent walks over to where Niels is sitting. He glances at the ribbons of duct tape holding Niels to the wooden chair.

"Your dad is nobody—by the time he figures it out you'll be worm food. Once we get the money I'm gonna pitch you over the cliff into the water—laugh as you fall headfirst onto the rocks below—very sharp rocks I might add. Blood will be everywhere when they find your body after they come searching."

He watches the reaction on the little boy's face and begins laughing loudly. He points at Niels and laughs even louder.

"Face it kid—you're already dead. You just don't know it yet—no one knows you're here. No one cares a lick for you."

Niels looks at the duct tape binding his arms.

7
University of the Virgin Islands

"You look like you've just seen a ghost or something?"

Omar turns around to look at Colin Rossmore as he drops a stack of medical books on top of the kitchen counter of his plantation-style dorm room. Omar shakes his head and sighs.

"Got a lot on my mind—plenty of drama."

Colin gestures with her hand.

"What's her name?"

Omar seems annoyed.

"It doesn't matter—it's over—finished."

He walks toward the balcony. He stops and faces Colin.

"How about we go for a drive? See a movie?"

Colin looks at the stack of books.

"No can do—got lots of studying to do."

Omar wrings his hands nervously and shrugs.

"OK—whatever—I'll see you later."

Colin watches as Omar heads to the door. He sighs.

"Don't do anything stupid."

Omar gives Colin a strange look and leaves.

"Uh-huh—I bet he got some chick pregnant. That's what happens when you don't use a condom—he's such an idiot."

He glances at the stack of books again.

8
Royal Dane Mall

"I thought you said Isabel Black was nothing to you. Not worth your time—couldn't be bothered if I recall right."

Cliff Nickerson seems irritated as he looks at Wendy Crowe and shrugs. He gestures with his hand and sighs.

"That bitch called me out—told everyone I was trying to score with some skanky girls from Antilles School—made me look like a geek—people are talking because of what she said."

Wendy rolls her eyes as they turn away from an ice cream stand. She grabs Cliff's arm. They look at each other.

"So what—no one listens to anything she says anyway. Her rep is terrible. Everyone knows she's a frigid virgin."

Cliff clenches his fist.

"I'm gonna get her. Teach her a lesson."

Wendy licks the ice cream cone in her hand and sighs.

"I'd leave it be if I were you. She's trouble."

She leans closer to him.

"I heard she likes girls."

Cliff turns to look at Wendy.

"I don't give a fuck if she's into girls—she needs to learn what happens when she messes with me. I want her to pay."

He clenches his fist again and grimaces.

9

Niels nervously watches as Brent leaves the shack. As the door slams shut he begins pushing his chair back and forth.

"Those guys are such fools. Do they think I'm just gonna wait for them to kill me? Adults are idiots—uh-huh—idiots."

He grins as the edges of the duct tape binding his hands begin to fray as he pulls harder. The door opens suddenly.

"Yeah—that brat knows he's toast."

Brent laughs as Derek Ving follows him into the shack. They look at Niels and begin laughing. They point at him.

"I hope your parents can have another brat."

Niels watches as they circle him.

"Your days are numbered kid—DOA."

They begin laughing loudly as they look out the window at the ocean in a distance. Derek smirks and faces Niels again.

"You won't even make the local news."

Niels remains silent as they circle him once more and then leave the shack again. As the door closes Niels looks at his hands for a few seconds as the duct tape continues to fray at the edges while he forces the tape to stretch even further. He smirks.

10

As several reporters walk past him Scott walks over to Sandra with a huge grin on his face. He notices her glare.

"What's wrong? Did someone say something wrong? Bash your writing? If looks could kill—what the hell happened?"

Sandra angrily jabs Scott. He notices.

"Hey, what's going on?"

Sandra jabs him again and sighs.

"Who is she?"

Scott seems confused.

"Who are you talking about?"

Sandra grabs Scott by the arm. He winces.

"What did that woman want? Did she make a play for you—ask you out on a date? Did you accept her vile offer?"

Scott begins laughing and grins.

"What if I did? She knows techniques—went into graphic detail about blowjobs—left nothing to my imagination."

Page **127**

Sandra seems hurt and jabs Scott once more.

"We're *so* done—do you hear me—*done.*"

Scott pulls Sandra toward him. A huge grin creases his face. He laughs again seeing her reaction and points at her.

"I like it when you're jealous."

He makes a lewd gesture with his finger.

"Uh-huh—that's right—you just showed your cards—we both know I'm something special—worth having in your bed."

He waves his hand in the air seeing Sandra's rage. He reaches out to tousle her hair and gently kisses her neck.

"Relax already. That was a local television reporter named Shelby Wilkins. She wanted to know if I could swing getting her an interview with you—loves your book—enjoyed it."

Sandra seems to relax and smiles.

"She wasn't hitting on you?"

Scott wags his finger at Sandra and laughs.

"No—all she did was talk about your book. She talked to Justin's secretary earlier but got blown off—thought she could have better luck with me—being your hot husband and all."

Sandra gives Scott a knowing look.

"I guess I jumped to conclusions. It just looked like she was trying to get you into her bed—making a play for you."

Scott pulls Sandra toward him.

"Well, I am an attractive guy if truth be told. Women like me—thinks I'm all that—always wanting to get into my pants to sample my wares—see if I'm as special as I appear to be."

Sandra jabs Scott playfully.

"Can you ego get any larger?"

Scott laughs and kisses Sandra.

"She liked my ripped jeans by the way."

Sandra shakes her fist at Scott.

"You're threading on thin ice dear husband—if I were you I'd watch your step—terrible things could happen when you least expect. I'm not a shrinking violet in case it slipped your mind."

Scott makes a lewd gesture with his finger again.

"Is that your way of threatening me?"

Page **128**

Sandra slides her finger across his belt buckle.

"Make it what you wish."

Scott leans closer to Sandra.

"What if I told you that one of the hotel maids made a play for me—asked if I could deliver? Said she didn't care if I was married to a famous writer—said she'd willingly share me."

Sandra shoots Scott a warning look.

"Nice try—but the maids come by when we're out—they couldn't have met you—couldn't have made such an offer."

Scott gestures with his hand.

"OK—OK—I lied."

Sandra hugs Scott and seems about to cry.

"I couldn't handle it if you cheated."

Scott reaches out to touch Sandra's cheek lightly. He points to the ring on his finger and waves it around.

"See this ring—I'm a married man—I promised you I wouldn't cheat and I haven't even thought of it. But I never promised I wouldn't tease you endlessly or enjoy pissing you off royally. I love those perks—love watching you get mad."

Sandra hugs Scott tightly.

"I don't know what I'd do without you."

Scott grins as he sees Justin coming toward them.

11

Bordeaux Road

"Are you serious Caleb? We have to walk to Santa Maria Beach through the woods? Ugh—what if there are bugs?"

Abigail Gluck stands defiantly with her hands on her hips as Caleb Farrow turns around to face her. He seems annoyed.

"I told you there wasn't a paved road to the beach. We have to walk down a path—my brother said it was right over there to the right—said the path was easy to find—oh-oh—*huh*."

Caleb reacts as he sees a foot sticking out from some thorny bushes less than ten feet away from the trail. He gasps.

"Is that what I think it is? Is that a body?"

Page **129**

Right behind him Abigail stops abruptly and watches in shock as Caleb gingerly takes a cautious step forward.

"Do you think she was raped?"

Caleb turns to face Abigail.

"I don't know—can't tell—most of her body is hidden under the bushes. But she seems pretty beat up though."

Less than a second later Abigail pulls out her cell phone and begins dialing. As she dials she watches Caleb as he takes another stop closer toward the thorny shrubbery. He sighs.

12

As multiple photographers prepare to take a mash of pictures Justin seems nervous as he faces Sandra and Scott.

"This will be just one of many to come."

Behind them Victoria de Hoya, Diana Munroe and Armand Bell smile endlessly as flashes erupt in the small bookstore while nearby Maxwell Pendergraft, John Smythe, Boris Birney and Peter Zimmerman are standing, waiting for their pictures to be taken. Among the people standing nearby with signed books in their hands are Casey Tyverton and Marla Jefferson. Greg Sharpe is standing next to her seemingly bored. Victoria glances over at him several times and licks her lips. Their eyes meet briefly.

13
Boston

"I guess my son has been playing me for a fool these last few months—telling me he's been studying really hard."

William Sharpe angrily clenches his fist as he watches a news clip from CBS about Sandra King's book signing.

"I should've known—should've seen how close they had become recently—my selfish son and whore of a girlfriend."

He stands up and walks toward the window.

"The question is what am I going to do about it?"

He grins slyly and turns around.

Page **130**

"How can I inflict as much pain as possible in the process for the both of them—make sure they regret playing me?"

He leans against the window and looks out at the skyline below. He fingers angrily clench and unclench. He grins.

"Let's see how that two-timing son of mine feels about being left without a penny to his wretched name—no place to live and no future to speak of—yeah—I think his reactions will speak volumes when he finds out he's out on his own with nothing."

He begins laughing loudly and whistles.

"Of course there's the matter concerning Marla Jefferson and her betrayal of my trust. I was warned about her—several of my associates had plenty to say about her reputation. But like an idiot I trusted her—didn't listen to what was staring me right in the face for weeks now—my whore girlfriend and my son."

He walks back toward his desk and sits down.

"I think it's time I make my move."

He grabs his cell phone and begins dialing. As he slowly leans back in his chair he grins broadly and gestures.

14
Mandahl Bay Beach

"How soon are they gonna fork over the money for the brat—has his folks said anything since—called you back?"

Brent runs his fingers through his hair and faces Derek with a grimace. He glances at the cell phone in his other hand.

"No—from what Savannah said the place is crawling with cops—setting up all sorts of equipment to monitor calls."

Derek seems nervous as he sighs loudly.

"What if they've figured it out already? What if that sister of yours spilled her guts—told them about the two of us?"

Brent grabs Derek by the throat.

"Savannah wouldn't dare fink on me—she knows what I'd do to her if she crossed me. Besides, she's in this as much as we are. There's no way for her to clear herself—no way at all."

He releases his grip on Derek and sighs.

Page **131**

"That rotten kid is worth millions—I've been doing research on his pop. They're not Vanderbilt rich but they've got plenty of dough to toss around—the kid's great-grandfather was quite the businessman in Denmark—moved to the Caribbean just before Denmark sold the Virgin Islands to the United States."

Brent gestures with his hand and laughs as he looks back toward the shack in a distance. He looks at his cell phone.

"We'll sponge his folks and then throw the brat off the cliff onto the rocks—when they find him it'll be too late. They won't be able to save their kid—it'll serve him right for being such a snarky twerp that thinks he knows everything about life."

Derek looks out toward the ocean.

"I still don't trust your sister."

Brent clenches his fist.

"OK—fine—whatever dude—suit yourself."

He pulls out a handgun and grins.

15

Sandra and Scott are standing by a bookshelf as Justin walks by and gives them a cautious look. He smiles broadly.

"There's someone who wants to talk to you."

He watches Sandra's reaction.

"This isn't another reporter. I think you'll like this one without a doubt—and if you don't—you can shoot me later."

Sandra shakes her fist at Justin.

"I'll hold you to it."

She watches as Justin turns a large monitor around and snaps his fingers as the screen suddenly comes to life. Sandra gasps as she realizes what is happening. She seems pleased.

"Oh my God—Larisa—but I thought."

On the screen streaming directly from Ocean Landing is Larisa Lopez. She smiles broadly as she faces Sandra.

"I couldn't come—I'm sorry. I know I promised but Ward wouldn't let me. I'm being held prisoner—by my husband."

Without warning Ward Brady appears.

Page **132**

"Uh-huh—I'm a bad guy—I like keeping my gorgeous wife a prisoner—gotta to make sure she doesn't get away."

Larisa and Ward begin laughing.

"Actually, I was ordered not to fly on account of what I'm carrying—my doctor absolutely forbid it—laid down the law."

As Sandra watches Larisa stands up and reveals she's in the last months of pregnancy. Ward grins broadly and winks.

"Uh-huh—that's right I'm to blame for her condition and I'm not the least bit sorry for my actions—not in the least."

Sandra reaches out to touch the screen.

"Oh my God—I'm so happy for you guys—it's been so long since I saw the two of you. You must be so excited—ecstatic."

Larisa looks at Ward and smiles.

16
Frenchman's Reef Resort

"I can't believe Sandra's book is already being shopped as a movie in Hollywood—she'll be the envy of everyone."

Victoria slowly closes the door behind her and faces Maxwell with a sly grin on her face. She walks over to him.

"Scott is quite the scene stealer too—that man is eye candy without a doubt—he knows how to flaunt his charms."

Maxwell rolls his eyes and sighs.

"Scott Malone is a bore—the dude has no game."

Victoria slides her arm around Maxwell's waist and kisses him in the back of the neck. She tugs at his belt buckle.

"Uh-huh—I got it on good authority the two of you have become really good friends—like old college buddies."

Maxwell gestures with his hand.

"OK—OK—I like the guy. He's fun to be around—when he's not prancing around thinking he's something special."

Victoria begins to unzip Maxwell's jeans.

"I saw the way Diana Munroe looked at you."

Maxwell runs his fingers through his hair.

"She and I are friends—good friends actually."

Victoria gives Maxwell a knowing look.

"Is she and you the kind of friends you and I are?"

Maxwell grins broadly as he watches Victoria's hand slip inside his boxer briefs. He lets out a sigh as she begins stroking his swelling penis. He laughs as her fingers slide over the head.

"I'm a single guy—she's single as well."

Victoria rolls her eyes.

"I'm not casting stones at anyone—you have the right to engage in as much sexual activity as you deem necessary."

She pulls him closer to her.

"I'm just glad to have you in my bed."

Maxwell watches as she begins undressing him.

17
Blakely Mansion

"I thought I told you to lie low for a while—make waves and you'll blow everything. No one has said anything to me."

Savannah seems annoyed as she nervously walks back and forth on the balcony outside her room. She stops suddenly.

"Taking that kid was a mistake. His folks are combing the island as we speak—one wrong move and you'll get busted."

She sighs loudly and rolls her eyes.

"Like I told you before I don't know anything."

Savannah listens to Brent yelling on the other end of the line. His voice becomes more and more shrill. She shrugs.

"OK—go ahead and trip up your gameplay—but don't say I didn't warn you ahead—Viktor Anderssen is out for blood."

She nervously turns around again.

"Uh-huh—that's right—he's nobody's fool."

At that moment she realizes that Byron is standing less than twelve feet away from her. She reacts in shock.

"Who are you talking to?"

Savannah hastily shuts off her cell phone.

"No one—it was a wrong number."

Byron seems confused and takes a step closer.

"Didn't seem like no one to me—seemed like you knew who you were talking to. What's going on Savannah?"

Savannah turns away from Byron.

"Don't you have something else to do?"

Byron digs his hands into the front pockets of his shorts and glances at the phone in Savannah's hand. He takes another step as Savannah turns around. She twitches nervously.

"We'll talk about this later."

Byron glances at Savannah's cell phone again.

"Who were you *really* talking to earlier?"

Savannah looks at the open door leading to her room and then at Byron. She points to the door. He ignores her.

"Do you have a boyfriend?"

Savannah reacts and points to the door again. Byron watches as she walks to the door and waits. He smirks.

18
Denmark Hill

"I thought I warned you to stay away from Cliff Nickerson and his friends. They're bad news. Treats everyone at school like garbage—acts like he owns the world. Dude is a prick."

Hadley Black runs his fingers through his hair and turns to face the winding staircase leading to the mansion perched against the hill less than a hundred feet away. Isabel Black waves her hand in the air and seems annoyed. Hadley grimaces.

"If he comes near you again I think you should get a restraining order—scare him a bit. I guarantee it isn't the first time some girl had to force that bastard to leave her alone."

He watches as Isabel leans against his car.

"He has the most sordid rep at school when it comes to how he treats a girl after he's fucked her. According to what my friends have heard he has even played doctor with Whitney's older sister—there are stories about him hooking up with her at a sports bar at Havensight—the one with a lot of prostitutes."

Hadley makes a lewd gesture with his finger.

"One of my friends told me she saw him at a free clinic in Frenchtown two weeks ago—the one that caters to druggies and homeless people that hang in the area—likely STD scare."

Isabel glances at her cell phone.

"Hadley, you don't have to worry about me falling for the lies Cliff Nickerson spouts—I already told him to get lost."

Hadley notices the name on Isabel's phone.

"What does she want?"

Isabel shrugs and begins talking.

19
Television Station

"Are you sure? Someone found a body of a young woman out near Santa Maria Beach? Was it murder or a suicide?"

Curtis Marlowe shakes his head as he hastily grabs a video camera and follows Shelby Wilkins out the door in a rush.

"The police are already there on the scene from what I heard—a young couple apparently stumbled upon the body."

Shelby follows Curtis into the parking lot.

20
Mafolie Hotel

"It was so nice of Larisa and Ward to call. They seem so happy—he's such a wonderful husband—really loves her."

Scott rolls his eyes and walks toward the balcony and looks out at the harbor. Sandra comes toward him.

"I'm still mad at you."

Scott turns around and seems confused.

"I thought I explained what happened earlier?"

Sandra slides her arms around Scott's waist and pulls him toward her. She looks into his eyes and kisses him lightly.

"I won't tolerate you shamelessly flirting—being charming and incredibly handsome is working against you in the worst way—wearing your favorite pair of jeans is a problem too."

Page **136**

Scott looks down at his snug-fitting Levi's and laughs as Sandra begins tugging at the buttons. She pushes him against the railing. He seems nervous and looks around cautiously.

"Hey—be really careful—dangerous situation involving a royally pissed off wife and her extremely attractive hubby."

Scott grins broadly and wags his finger at Sandra.

"I'm not sorry I flirted—she liked me."

Sandra jabs Scott playfully.

"Uh-huh—in case you forgot I'm your wife and I intend to get even—wipe that smirk off your face—totally erase it."

Scott gestures with his hand as Sandra pulls him away from the balcony. She points toward the bedroom. He grins and lets himself be led down the hallway—whistling loudly.

21
Bordeaux Road

"The coroner already left? Damn it—must be a really slow day if they're quick on the take. I wonder what happened."

Curtis looks over to where a small crowd is gathered. He points toward a trail as several police officers come from the clearing. Shelby shakes her head and slowly follows him.

22
Boston

"Uh-huh—that's right. I'm a ball-buster. If that loser won't acknowledge he fathered your unborn baby I'll set your plan in motion immediately—break Cliff Nickerson's jelly spine."

Jeremy Winterfield leans back in his chair and nods several times as a huge grin spreads across his face. He leans forward.

"Young Nickerson won't know what hit him. His pop is gonna face reality whether he wants to or not. I've got a rep scaring people into doing the right thing. I take no prisoners."

He begins laughing as he looks at Lindsay Ganz staring back at him with her father sitting next to her. She sighs.

"I didn't want to force the issue—but he refuses to admit what he did to me—pretends he's not the father. But he was the only guy I ever slept with—forced himself on me. Said he loved me—told me we'd be together forever. He promised me."

Jeremy leans closer to the monitor.

"He forced himself on you?"

Lindsay nods and looks at her father. Albert Ganz clenches his fist several times. He seems in shock at the revelation.

"Uh-huh—said I couldn't get pregnant."

Jeremy notices Albert's reaction. His reaction changes immediately as a gigantic smile spreads across Jeremy's face. He snaps his fingers as Lindsay and Albert look at each other.

"I think a rape charge might put a scare into young Nickerson. This is gonna get really messy quickly. He's going to have some serious financial issues by this time tomorrow."

Lindsay and Albert nod in agreement.

"What sort of work does his father do for a living?"

"I think he's a doctor."

Jeremy jumps up from his chair.

"He *was* a doctor. Having a rapist for a son will put a crimp on the reputation of the hospital that employs his father."

Jeremy glances at the window nearby. He snaps his fingers again and grabs a pad of paper nearby. He sighs.

"I'll call you tomorrow morning. Eight o'clock sharp."

The screen goes blank seconds later.

23
Main Street

Omar seems nervous as he walks aimlessly along the street. He stops a few times as if expecting someone to be following him. Several people look at him oddly. He sighs.

"That bitch had it coming. She was vile—no one will be sorry when they find out she's dead—least of all Lindsay."

He notices an electronics store up ahead with a large monitor in the window. Omar reacts as he faces the monitor.

"I guess *they* know. But there are no ties to me. I'll just play it cool for a couple of days. No one saw what I did."

He runs his fingers through his hair.

24
Frenchman's Reef Resort

Maxwell grins broadly as he stands in front of the elevator as time seems to stand still. He rubs his hand as if a bit chilled. He looks at his watch. Seconds later the door opens. He reacts in shock as he sees Tiffany Johnson standing inside the elevator.

25
Water Island

"Oh my God—no—it can't be. Not Ava."

Whitney Wilkins looks at her sister standing a few feet away from her. Shelby takes a step forward and shrugs.

"They found her less than an hour ago."

She watches her sister's reaction.

"She was murdered. Viciously strangled—I assume—from what I was told. Her neck was broken. She put up a fight—but nevertheless she was killed. There are no suspects at the moment from what the cops said—her parents have been told."

Whitney seems frozen in shock.

"But I just talked to her earlier today. She was in one of her usual moods—complaining about Lindsay Ganz ruining Cliff Nickerson's life. Said she was gonna get Lindsay—said she had a plan to help Cliff—said she'd call me tonight with the details. I can't believe something like that could happen to someone like her. Ava had lots of issues—but who would want to kill her."

Shelby shakes her head and reaches out to her sister. They hug for a few seconds as Whitney begins to cry.

"Was she raped?"

They look at each other.

"I don't think so—I assume not."

Whitney wipes a tear from her eye and sighs loudly.

"We had our differences—Ava could be a bitch when she wanted to be—but I liked her—we had a lot in common."

Shelby nods and hugs Whitney again.

"They'll catch who did it—this is a small island—where can they go? She must have known her killer—at least that's what one of the cops told me—didn't think she was killed by a stranger."

Whitney seems bothered by the statement.

26
Mandahl Bay Beach

"Yeah—uh-huh—that's right kid. Time's almost up. It's just a matter of time before you take a flying header off the cliff."

Niels looks at Derek and seems about to laugh.

"My dad will hunt you down and kill you."

Derek is about to hit Niels as he hears a noise outside and turns around. He walks to the window and peeks out but sees nothing. Seconds later there is a knocking sound. Niels begins to pull harder on the duct tape as Derek slowly opens the door.

"What the fuck is going on?"

There is a gust of air as the door slams shut. Derek tries to pull the door open. He seems in shock as the handle begins to frost over. As he looks at the doorknob curiously it changes back to normal. He grabs it again and opens the door once more.

"What the hell just happened?"

There is another sound and as he turns around Niels hits him with a piece of wood and runs past him. Derek appears to be stunned for a few seconds and then makes his way toward a worn path along the edge of a cliff nearby. As he runs in a panic he doesn't realize his peril and as he tries to grab hold of Niels he slips. He screams in terror as he realizes his error and desperately grabs hold of a few shrubs growing through the sharp rocks.

"Give me a hand kid—I'm gonna fall."

Niels stands several feet away and seems unable to move as he watches Derek's hand slipping. Derek screams.

"Help me or I'll kill you—I swear I will."

Niels watches in slow motion as Derek's hand slips even further and a panicked look spreads across his face. He tries to grab at the remaining shrubbery but to no avail. In a distance he hears a car pulling up. He looks at Niels again and grimaces.

"You can't let me die kid—help me."

Niels stands motionless as he watches Derek. He finally takes a step forward. Derek looks at him and grins broadly.

"That's right kid. Give me your hand."

At that moment Niels hears footsteps and someone calling out his name. He turns to look in the direction of the voice as Derek's hand slips further. Without warning he loses his grip and falls. He screams in terror as he plummets headfirst into the sharp boulders below. There is a loud scream and then silence. As Niels is about to look over the cliff he sees Maxwell running toward him. They look at each other for a few seconds.

"Niels Anderssen?"

Niels nods and seems afraid.

"*Who are you?*"

Maxwell takes a step forward and sighs loudly.

"Maxwell Pendergraft. I'm with the FBI."

Niels turns to look toward the rocks below as he catches a glimpse of a teenage girl standing about forty feet away with her hands on her hips and a huge smile on her face. He blinks and she's gone. He shakes his head and faces Maxwell again.

"How did you find me?"

Maxwell takes another step forward and shrugs.

"You wouldn't believe me if I told you."

Niels looks at Maxwell oddly.

"What kind of an answer is that?"

Maxwell grins broadly.

"How about we talk about it later OK—right about now I think we ought to get you back to your parents. Let's go."

Niels backs away from Maxwell. He looks back at where he saw the teenage girl—and at the cliff. Maxwell notices.

"Come on—this is no time to play games."

Niels raises his hand and points.

"How do I know you're with the FBI? You might be one of *them*. One of Brent's stupid friends—where *is* he anyway?"

Maxwell runs his fingers through his hair.

"You know his name?"

Niels nods several times.

"Duh—those bozos didn't even try to hide who they were and what they wanted. Those dummies actually thought I was Byron Blakely when they grabbed me—told me so anyway."

Maxwell pulls out his cell phone.

"Who are you calling?"

Maxwell turns to face Niels again.

27
Nickerson Mansion

Sounds of a car driving away can be heard as the front door closes. Travis Nickerson seems confused as he looks at the large green envelope in his hand. He slowly begins to open it.

"What the fuck is this?"

He pulls the flap open and pulls out a thick folder. He opens it cautiously and reacts as he sees the words NICKERSON vs. GANZ spelled out. He begins flipping through the folder. He clenches his fist and looks toward the hallway leading to a guest house in the backyard of his expansive home. He slowly walks down the hallway and as he walks past a pool he begins walking faster. Seconds later he is standing at the front door of the guest house. He sighs loudly as he continues to clench his fist.

"Cliff? I want to talk to you."

There is no answer. He knocks on the door.

"I know you're home—show your face this instant."

Seconds tick by and finally Cliff opens the door clad in a towel. He runs his fingers through his wet hair. He shrugs.

"What's the big deal—what's wrong?"

Travis seems about to explode as he shoves the folder toward Cliff. He points to it as Cliff looks at the folder.

Page **142**

"Who the hell is Lindsay Ganz?"

Cliff shrugs and seems bored by the topic. He shakes his head and looks down at the towel wrapped around his waist.

"She's nobody—just some girl I scored with a while back at Patrick's party. She's a whore—she got played. End of story."

Travis angrily grabs Cliff by the arm.

"Uh-huh—did she really? Or it is you that got played by that girl? Seems to me you should've thought about that before you decided to poke her. That girl is smarter than you think."

He pulls Cliff closer and grimaces.

"She's got a lawyer—one of the worst a businessman like me can come across if truth be known. She's suing you for half of everything you have. Her lawyer has his ducks in a row."

Cliff seems confused.

"It's not mine—she a slut. Ask anyone."

Travis pushes Cliff backwards.

"What happens when they do a DNA test smart guy?"

Cliff makes a lewd gesture with his finger.

"I'm not gonna give them a sample—they've got nothing on me—it's her word against mine. She's nothing—a zero."

Travis points his finger at Cliff.

"How stupid are you? They already have your medical records. Like I said, the lawyer that girl hired is no one's fool. First thing he did today was secure your medical records—and then he filed the paperwork. When he's through dragging you through the courts you won't have two nickels to rub together."

Cliff looks at the towel wrapped around his waist again. Travis notices and seems irritated and faces the mansion.

"Jeremy Winterfield has a solid reputation of destroying anyone who crosses him. A while back he sued this guy named Carson Penney after his son ran someone off the road."

Cliff rolls his eyes mockingly.

"I didn't rape that whore—I didn't have to."

Travis spins around to face Cliff again.

"Winterfield crucified Penney and his son without mercy. Penney suffered a fatal heart attack from what I heard."

He lowers his voice and seems scared. Cliff notices.

"I'm not afraid of some hack lawyer. I'll show him who's the boss—I'll make him see the light. Then I plan to teach Lindsay a lesson she won't forget—ruin her rep all over this island."

Travis angrily grabs Cliff again.

"How stupid are you son? Winterfield is going to crush you and destroy everything I've spent my life building. He's out for blood and intends to make me beg. I'll be lucky to keep this house when he's finished. After Carson Penney's death courtesy of Winterfield, his estate was completely drained of every last cent leaving nothing for the surviving Penney children. Last I heard they're living in some little town in Maine with their housekeeper. No future to speak of because of what their selfish older brother did—Winterfield and his reputation should be royally feared."

Cliff jerks free of his father's grip.

"What happened to the older brother?"

Travis seems about to laugh.

28
Mafolie

"What about the person on the phone?"

Maxwell turns to look at Niels sitting across from him in his car. He sighs loudly and pulls to a stop. Niels shrugs.

"I think it was a woman."

Maxwell looks at Niels curiously as he watches several cars zip by. He runs his fingers through his hair as Niels notices.

"Do you know for sure?"

Niels nods as Maxwell glances nervously at his cell phone for a few seconds. He seems annoyed and faces Niels again.

"How come you didn't mention that earlier?"

Niels rolls his eyes knowingly.

"I only remembered just now. That bozo kept yelling at someone on his phone all the time—saying if he got caught they would go down with him as well—seemed really freaked on kidnapping the wrong kid—threatened to kill me endlessly."

Maxwell wipes sweat from his brow.

"For a little boy you're really smart. Are you in advanced classes at school? You seem to have a grasp for adult stuff more than the average kid your age. Do you watch the news?"

Niels stifles a laugh.

"Uh-huh—I'm in advanced classes at my school. I watch the news too—cartoons are stupid—terrible writing."

Maxwell laughs and points at Niels.

"When I was a kid I liked *Scooby-Doo*. I also liked the *Charlie Brown* holiday specials. Those were the days."

Niels shakes his head and laughs.

"That's a bunch of kid stuff—I only watch smart television like *National Geographic* and *Discovery*. I'm a big fan of science."

Niels gives Maxwell a cautious look and then grabs his arm. They look at each other. Niels lowers his voice.

"When we were at the shack earlier—I saw something watching. Someone actually—it was a girl—a teenage girl."

Maxwell shoots Niels a nervous look.

"I didn't see anyone?"

Niels looks at Maxwell directly.

"I know what I saw at the beach. There was a girl standing with her hands on her hips—she seemed pleased with herself for some reason—had a smug look on her face—then gone."

Maxwell looks at the little boy curiously.

"You must have imagined it. There was no one else at the beach but us—certainly not a teenage girl—impossible."

Niels defiantly points his finger at Maxwell.

"I know what I saw."

Maxwell seems bothered and looks away. Niels pulls out a piece of paper from his pants pocket. With a pencil he begins sketching what he saw. Maxwell reacts and sighs loudly.

TO BE CONTINUED

A Brief Look at the Sixth Episode

Nothing is what it seems when several events play out with tragic results for more than one person as a little boy experiences a strange visit that leaves an impression while a sadistic kidnapper resumes hunting his prey unaware he's also being hunted.

Glass Houses

1
Market Square

Alexis de Hoya seems annoyed as he looks at his father while he chomps down on a sandwich. He sighs as he notices a few of his classmates walk by. Alexander de Hoya grimaces.

"How long are you going to play this game?"

They stare at each other for a few seconds.

"I wasn't aware I was playing a game?"

Alexis watches his father closely. He seems about to lose his patience as he slowly runs his fingers through his hair.

"Exactly what do you want from me? You shamelessly disrespected my mother with that whore—lied to me."

Alexander wipes sweat from his brow.

"Your mother and I were already having issues before things went south—we were already headed for splitsville."

Alexis gives his father a harsh look.

"That excuse doesn't change anything."

Alexander gestures with his hand.

"I never said it did. But I *am* your father regardless."

Alexis rolls his eyes and leans back in his chair.

"Don't pull that **Bing Crosby** stance on me. He was a lousy father. Ruined the lives of his sons—all of them—made *Mommie Dearest* by **Christina Crawford** look tame by comparison."

Alexander clenches his fist and sighs.

"Don't bring up that awful man's name to me. He and I are nothing alike. I've made mistakes—tried to patch things."

Alexis leans forward in his chair.

"Look, I'm aware of your mistakes, all of them, never expected a perfect father. But cheating is an egregious act."

He reduces his voice to a whisper.

"When you figure out how to say you're sorry—and mean it—let me know—until then I think you and I have nothing more to talk about at the moment. Enjoy the flight back to San Juan."

Alexander reacts as Alexis stands and walks away. As he watches his son walk toward the door of the diner he notices several people looking at him and whispering to each other.

2

Mafolie

Maxwell Pendergraft looks at the sketch in his hand and seems about to faint. He stares at the drawing and then turns to look at Niels Anderssen. Niels grins broadly and gestures.

"That's the girl I saw."

Maxwell sighs loudly as he looks at the drawing again and blinks a few times. He turns to look at Niels seconds later.

"Don't tell anyone about this, OK? Let it go."

Niels snatches the drawing away from Maxwell.

"Why not—why shouldn't I say anything?"

Maxwell runs his fingers through his hair and shrugs.

"Just don't say anything—forget what you saw."

Niels gives Maxwell a curious look and grins.

"She's a ghost, isn't she? That's why you don't want me to say anything. It's because people will say I'm crazy. Say that I've been seeing things that aren't there. Uh-huh—that's it."

Page 148

Niels looks at the drawing as Maxwell grimaces.

"I bet I can find out who she was through the Internet in an hour. I bet she was trying to help me—made sure I escaped."

Maxwell reacts and faces Niels. He watches as the little boy traces his finger over the sketch. They look at each other.

"How old are you again?"

"I'm eight."

Maxwell shakes his head.

"Are you sure? You seem like twenty to me. How do you know so much? What are they teaching you in school?"

Niels grins broadly.

"I'm smarter than everyone I know—including you."

He grabs Maxwell by the arm and sighs.

"Do you think that girl I saw was a ghost?"

Maxwell turns away and sighs.

"Do you think she knew who I was and tried to stop those two bozos from killing me earlier—made Derek see her?"

Maxwell glances at the drawing again.

"I don't know—I didn't see anything. But if I were you I'd keep what you saw to yourself. Best you don't tell anyone."

Niels shoots Maxwell a curious look.

"Not even my parents?"

Maxwell grimaces.

"Don't tell anyone—not your parents—not the cops—not your friends—no one can know what you saw at the beach."

Niels seems confused at the statement.

3
Nickerson Mansion

"I know all that already—but it's too late to cry about it now. What can I do to stop that Winterfield dude from taking me to the cleaners—he's got a troubling reputation when it comes to taking guys like—he's drawn a line in the sand—left no doubt whatsoever that he intends to crucify Cliff—destroy him."

Travis Nickerson looks at the cell phone in his hand.

Page **149**

"I have no idea what to expect until he makes his next move—made it clear he intends to make an example out of Cliff refusing to accept responsibility for his recent behavior."

Travis stops and faces the balcony a few feet away.

"Isn't there anything you can do? Curb Winterfield before he can destroy Cliff's life. He has to have skeletons in his closet. A man like him doesn't get where he is by staying pure."

He runs his fingers through his hair.

"Yes—yes—I'll see what my investigators can dig up. See where I stand with the Ganz family. It's worth a try to call their bluff and see what they really want—a sweet payoff certainly would silence them—obstruct their motives outright."

He grins broadly and nods.

"Uh-huh—why didn't I think of that idea before—love the concept no doubt. They'll never suspect a thing—love it."

Travis nods in agreement a few times.

4
Mafolie Hotel

"I don't know what I'd do if you weren't in my life."

Scott Malone laughs as he looks at Sandra King lying in his arms, tangled between several blankets. He kisses her softly.

"Uh-huh—right back at you."

Sandra reaches out to tousle Scott's hair.

"Larisa and Ward said we should visit them—said we should make plans to spend a week in Ocean Landing."

Scott begins to laugh as he pulls her tightly against his chest. He gently slides his finger across her cheek and grins.

"I see where this is going—and while we're there pay your parents an impromptu visit too. Have your mother lay a guilt trip on me for not putting a baby in you. Tell you how much she wants to be a grandmother—how much it would mean to her."

Sandra shakes her finger at Scott.

"My mother likes you—said you were perfect for me. Said I needed a guy that kept me on my toes—wasn't boring."

Page 150

Scott sits up in bed. He wags his finger at Sandra.

"I like your mother too—we get along really well. Took her to that salsa dance contest the last time we visited."

Sandra jabs Scott in the chest.

"You kept the fact you can dance salsa from me. Said I was on a need-to-know basis. I'm still mad if you must know."

Scott laughs again and kisses Sandra.

5
Anderssen Estate

Maxwell watches as Valerie Anderssen hugs Niels warmly as several men in black jackets glance at where Maxwell is standing. A few feet away Viktor Anderssen eyes Maxwell with a curious stare. He walks toward him seconds later and shrugs.

"Exactly how did you find where my son was being held captive? Niels claims you just showed up at the beach?"

Maxwell runs his fingers through his hair.

"I guess I was in the right place at the right time."

Viktor looks at Maxwell oddly.

6
Mountain Top

Brent Crawford slams his fist against the steering wheel of his jeep as he looks at the footage of Niels with his parents.

"Damn Derek for being so careless—who the fuck is that guy. How did he know where to find that miserable kid?"

He looks at the news footage again.

"Of course—*Savannah*—that damn sister of mine turned on me even after she promised. She's gonna pay—pay dearly."

He angrily clenches his fist and grimaces.

"I'm going to teach her a lesson."

He begins to laugh and shuts off his cell phone.

"Seems to me she chose which side she's playing for—but that will be her undoing—she's a dead woman walking."

He grins as he glances at the gun sticking out of the glove compartment. Brent reaches to grab it and smirks. He slides his fingers over the barrel and begins laughing hysterically.

"That sister of mine is as good as dead—and then I'll deal with Astrid and that guy she thinks is her white knight. Let's see how Peter Zimmerman handles being shot by yours truly."

He kisses the gun several times and sighs.

One Day Later

7
Denmark Hill

Isabel Black gets into her car and drives away. Behind her Cliff Nickerson grins broadly as he begins following her.

"No one will be there to save her from the likes of me. That bitch is gonna know what it feels like to get played."

He laughs as he watches her drive toward a narrow road leading up a nearby mountain. Cliff clenches his fist as he watches Isabel weave and dodge along the narrow road. He shrugs.

"She shouldn't have crossed me—shouldn't have told tales about me—made me look bad to my friends—insulted my rep."

He smirks as he watches her come to a stop.

8
Windward Passage Hotel

Silas Bell pulls the door shut to his hotel room and begins walking down the hallway. As he turns the corner he sees Diana Munroe coming toward him. Their eyes meet briefly.

9
Mafolie

Cliff jumps out of his car and runs toward Isabel's car as she pulls to a stop. His rage is evident as he grabs her arm.

"You and I have some unfinished business to attend to pertaining to the trash you said about me to my friends."

Isabel tries to free herself from Cliff's grip.

"Let go of me this instant or I'll scream."

Cliff begins laughing.

"Go ahead—no one will hear you. Frigging road is deserted this time of morning. Besides, who would stop and help you—you're nothing but a conniving whore that has crossed the wrong guy. It's time for us to dance—see what happens."

He angrily forces Isabel out of the car.

10

Back Street Cafe

"Word on the street is you're a big-time hero. Rescuing some rich kid makes for a spin in the news cycle. What's it like being the darling of the media all of a sudden? How many dates have you lined up just because your face has been splashed all over television? Do tell? Inquiring minds want to know."

Maxwell wags his finger at Scott.

"Don't you get started on me this morning Scotty—don't need your kind of insults. It's already been plenty weird."

He takes a sip of coffee from his mug.

"I just happened to luck out where that boy is concerned. The whole island is being turned upside down trying to find the one that got away. Kid seemed to think there were three instead of two—said he overheard several phone conversations."

Scott rolls his eyes knowingly.

"Exactly how old is that boy again?"

Maxwell gestures with his hand and shrugs.

11

Cliff tries to force Isabel into the backseat of his car as she struggles to push him away. He reaches out to hit her just as a car comes into view. Seconds later he's grabbed from behind.

Page **153**

Anderssen Estate

"Did you think you were gonna die? Was it scary?"

Niels shakes his head and turns to face the window as Byron Blakely gives him a curious look. He stands up.

"Did you see their gun? What kind was it?"

Niels faces Byron and shrugs. He seems focused on something else as Byron walks toward where Niels in standing.

"Did you see the guy fall off the cliff?"

Niels glances toward the door.

"No—it all happened so fast. He just slipped and fell from the cliff—and—there was—but I only heard him scream."

He watches Byron's reaction.

"They had me tied up—they threatened to kill me—but didn't get the chance to do it. Then something happened."

Byron seems confused.

"What are you talking about?"

Niels shakes his head and gestures.

13

Police Station

"This is an outrage. I want to see my boy this minute."

Travis clenches his fist as he looks at the rookie police officer standing behind a desk. He leans forward—making sure the officer is the only one who can hear him whispering.

"I'm going to have your badge young man. You'll be lucky if you can get a job as a dog catcher in this frigging island."

The officer, Steve Snell, calmly looks at Travis and at the lobby in front of him. He gives Travis a knowing and sighs.

"There are no dog catcher jobs on St. Thomas. That was *so* 1970s. We've moved on sir—dogs are micro-chipped."

Travis seems enraged and turns around to face the lobby.

"Do you know I am? I'm rich—very rich. Is that clear?"

Steve rolls his eyes and turns away. Travis is about to pound his fist on the counter as he sees a police officer coming from the nearby hallway. He rushes over and notices Isabel talking to another officer in a locked room. He grimaces.

"I'm Travis Nickerson. I want to see my son."

Antonio Macron seems annoyed and ushers Travis toward an empty room. He shuts the door and coldly faces Travis.

"Your son is being held on two counts. The first being an assault on one Isabel Black—the other is suspicion of murder."

Travis reacts and grabs Antonio's arm.

"Assault—murder—what the fuck are you talking about? My son is an upstanding member of society—a winner."

Antonio looks at Travis cautiously as he releases the grip on his arm. He hands Travis a folder. He wags his finger at Travis as he watches him begin to flip through the thick blue folder.

"It seems your son—to use your words—an upstanding member of society—had been charged in the assault of Isabel Black as witnessed by a passerby who intervened and restrained your son until police arrived. Unfortunately, there's the more pressing matter concerning the tragic murder of Ava Fontaine yesterday. It seems prior to her death by strangulation she was sexually assaulted—semen found in her vagina matches samples supplied by your son last year involving your housekeeper. I think you'd better call your lawyer—this is gonna get messy."

Travis seems about to explode.

"My housekeeper lied outright—there was no assault—she was a willing participant—admitted as much at the trial."

Antonio shakes his head and points to the door as Travis looks at the folder again. He walks to the door and stops.

"My son didn't kill anyone—he's being framed."

Antonio shrugs and points to the door again.

"If I had a dollar for everyone who spouted that line I'd be living in a beachfront home atop Peterborg Peninsula."

Travis shakes the folder at Antonio.

"Do you know I am? Know how wealthy?"

Antonio points to the door once more and sighs.

"I don't care if you're **John F. Kennedy Jr**. Your son is no different from anyone else as far as I'm concerned. Good day."

Travis shoots Antonio a nasty look and snarls.

"He's dead—in case you don't pay attention to the news. He's been dead for over two decades now—just saying."

Antonio ignores the comment and watches as Travis walks past him and enters the hallway. He shuts the door.

14
Windward Passage Hotel

"When is your flight back to Los Angeles scheduled?"

Diana looks over at Maxwell lying next to her in bed. She reaches out to tousle his hair. He grins and they kiss again.

"Six o'clock. Still plenty of time to play with my favorite guy—such a pity you can't come back with me—would make for an interesting flight. The mile high club would definitely be in play no doubt—put plenty of unruly celebrities to shame."

Maxwell laughs and wags his finger at Diana.

"Headed back to DC—got plenty of work waiting for me the moment I arrive. How about a rain check? Next year?"

Diana nods in agreement and reaches out to kiss Maxwell sensuously. They kiss passionately for a few minutes.

"I'm gonna miss you."

She strokes his cheek with her finger, then jabs Maxwell gently on the chest. He smirks as she points her finger at him.

"What about Victoria?"

Maxwell gives Diana a cautious look.

"What about her?"

Diana jabs Maxwell again.

"I'm not blind Maxwell dear—I saw how she looked at you at the signing for Sandra's book yesterday. She likes you."

Maxwell waves his hand in the air.

"We're just friends—good friends."

Diana wags her finger at him.

"Why can't you just give me a straight answer?"

Maxwell begins laughing loudly.

"I thought I did. We're friends—nothing more."

He pulls Diana toward him and kisses her. She kisses him back and looks at the door several feet away. She sighs.

"I bet you've got a few more really good friends in DC that keep you company on cold nights—plenty I assume."

Maxwell smirks and ignores her.

<h2 style="text-align:center">15</h2>

Niels sits at the window of his bedroom and watches as Byron walks through the gate that separates their homes.

"I bet he wishes he could trade places with me."

He shakes his head and as he turns around he reacts in shock upon realizing he's no longer alone in the room.

"How did you get in here?"

Tiffany Johnson laughs and takes a step forward.

"I can do anything I want—be anywhere."

Niels seems frozen in shock as he watches Tiffany closely and recognizes her. He raises his hand in the air and points.

"You're *her*—*you're* the girl at the beach."

Tiffany takes another step forward.

"You weren't supposed to see me yesterday."

Niels seems confused.

"What do you mean I wasn't supposed to see you at the beach? I saw you—saw you standing with your hands on your hips. You seemed pleased with yourself—happy almost."

Tiffany takes another step forward.

"Do you know why I'm here?"

Niels shakes his head.

"Can you walk through walls?"

Tiffany takes another step forward. She briefly glances back at the door and then faces Niels again. She shrugs.

"Is that all you can think of to ask me, Niels? Do you have any idea what's happening at this very moment? Do you?"

Niels slowly takes a step backwards.

Page 157

"Are you a ghost? How did you get past the security guards outside my door? How come they didn't see you?"

Tiffany laughs and raises her hand.

"You can't tell anyone about what you saw."

Niels gives Tiffany a curious look as she points toward the door while he watches in shocked amazement as icicles begin forming on the doorknob. His eyes widen as Tiffany grins.

"No one must ever know."

As Niels continues watching, ice completely covers the door. He seems afraid and looks at the window. He gasps.

"I think you should leave."

Tiffany points her finger at Niels.

"This must be our secret."

Niels waves his hand in the air.

"I didn't tell Byron. I could've but I didn't."

"I know."

Niels nervously looks at the window again.

"*What do you mean you know?*"

Tiffany snaps her fingers several times. As Niels watches the room suddenly seems awash in a cloudy mist. He reacts.

"Can you see the future?"

Tiffany gives Niels a knowing look.

"It depends."

Niels rubs his eyes and shrugs.

"There are no such things as ghosts."

Tiffany laughs and watches as the mist begins to swirl faster and faster. Niels watches in fascination as the mist seems to suddenly come alive. He looks around the room as hardly anything seems visible. It seems like only he and Tiffany are alone in the room. He seems unable to move as she comes closer.

16
Royal Dane Mall

"Have you visited Mysterious Island yet? I heard it has been completely transformed—almost harmless looking."

Sandra shakes her head as Shelby Wilkins takes a sip of coffee. They share a brief glance as several people walk by.

"There were plans in the works but my schedule suddenly took a different turn. My publisher booked several extra signings in Miami and Atlanta. I'm leaving the island later tonight."

Shelby seems disappointed and sighs loudly.

"Maybe next time will be the charm?"

Sandra nods and takes a sip of her iced coffee.

"Scott and I definitely intend to come back—heard plenty about some of the beaches—like a postcard—picturesque."

Shelby nods in agreement.

"Say goodbye for me to that charming husband of yours when you see him next. Such a nice guy—loves you—couldn't stop talking about how much he owes his happiness to you after everything that happened—made him feel like he could take on the world—said you're the only one that ever understood him."

Sandra grins broadly and gestures with her hand.

"It's he who deserves the thanks. There's never a dull moment with him—makes me laugh—charms me silly."

Shelby reaches out to touch Sandra's hand.

"I envy your life."

Sandra nods and takes another sip of coffee. Several people walk by and seem to recognize Shelby. She notices.

"I'll send you a copy when it's ready. Really appreciated having you meet with me. I've learned so much today."

Sandra nods again and stands up.

17
Boston

"Oh, this just gets better and better. Time to apply the screws and make Nickerson wince—uh-huh—I think he'll be ready to fork over piles of cash rather than go through a court battle with his son in the slammer for murder. Prep the paperwork in the next hour—seems to me this is the perfect time to play."

Jeremy Winterfield grins broadly and nods.

Page **159**

"Jack up the asking price and make it sixty-five percent of everything young Nickerson was entitled to before he decided to strangle one of his girlfriends—call Ganz with the good news."

Jeremy begins laughing as he looks at the news clips flashing across the screen from MSNBC. He grins slyly.

18

Niels watches in shock as several people emerge through the mists. His eyes bulge out of their sockets as he realizes what is happening. Through the mist **Abraham Lincoln** emerges with **Bob the Cat** sitting on his shoulder. Next to him **Pocahontas** stands proudly, clad in clothing from the Elizabethan era. **Wilbur Wright** emerges and is followed by his brother **Orville Wright**. As Niels continues to watch in shocked amazement **Anne Frank** and **Princess Diana** take their places next to the others. He turns to look at Tiffany and realizes she's right beside him. She raises her hand and points toward where the others are standing.

"As I said earlier you must not tell anyone what you saw at the beach yesterday—or in your room today. What you saw must remain a secret. Do you understand? No one must ever know."

Niels still seems in a daze. Tiffany reaches out to touch him. He suddenly takes a step backwards almost stumbling.

"I must be dreaming—this can't be happening."

Tiffany reaches out to touch Niels again.

"You're quite a special little boy—one with a bright future ahead of you. But you also have a gift—able to see things."

Niels rubs his eyes.

"What are you talking about?"

Tiffany glances at the others and then back at Niels.

"Do you know what's happening?"

Niels rolls his eyes and nods.

"I'm not a dummy. I've read a lot of books—plenty actually. I know who everyone here are—even the cat on Lincoln's shoulders. I read the book about him last year—saw the movie too. Why are they here? What's going on? Am I going to die?"

Page **160**

He glances over at where the apparitions are standing. He points and then faces Tiffany again. He rubs his eyes again.

"Did I do something wrong again? I'm always getting yelled at by adults. My parents don't know much of anything if you must know—I feel like I'm their teacher sometimes."

Tiffany shoots Niels a knowing look.

19
Mafolie Hotel

Sandra opens the door to her hotel room and sees Scott sitting in a chair on the balcony asleep. She walks over to him and gently kisses him on the cheek. He awakens and grins.

"How did the interview go?"

Sandra leans over and kisses Scott again.

"Just when I thought you couldn't do anything to make me love you even more—you pull yet another stunt."

Scott stands up and laughs.

"I deny whatever you're talking about."

Sandra pulls Scott toward her and kisses him again.

"You can't deny what you said."

Scott wags his finger at Sandra.

"Says who?"

Sandra pushes Scott against the sliding glass door.

"Shelby Wilkins told me what you said."

Scott grins broadly and pulls away from Sandra. He walks toward the kitchenette several feet away. Sandra follows.

"I said nothing. She's a liar."

Sandra corners Scott near the door and aggressively pulls him toward her again. He seems a bit nervous and grins slyly.

"It's her word against mine."

Sandra reaches out to stroke Scott's cheek. She seems pleased and strokes his cheek again. She kisses him lightly.

"You said it—every word of it."

Scott gestures with his hand as a smirk spreads across his face. He watches as Sandra playfully tugs at his belt buckle.

"I have no idea what you're talking about. I deny whatever was said. I'm just not the type of guy to say mushy stuff."

Sandra looks at Scott's belt buckle.

"You can't talk your way out of this situation—I won't let you—we both know Shelby Wilkins is telling the truth."

Scott grins broadly and turns away.

"I can and I will."

Sandra kisses Scott again.

"I demand you come clean right now."

Scott laughs again and presses his lips together.

"I have ways to make you spill your guts."

Scott looks at Sandra curiously.

"I don't respond to threats."

Sandra releases her grip on Scott.

"We'll see about that."

Without warning she begins tickling him. He bursts out laughing and begs for mercy as she intensifies her behavior.

"OK—OK—I admit it—every word of it."

Sandra seems about to cry.

"Do you know much I love you?"

Scott nods and pulls Sandra toward him. He looks at her and nods. They kiss for a few seconds. He grins broadly.

20
Reynolds Estate

Silas watches as Armand Bell kisses his son goodbye and shuts the door to the car. He watches as Jasmine Rossmore drives away seconds later. He doesn't see Silas sitting in his car just down the street. Less than a minute later Silas begins following Jasmine. He grins as he glances over at the gun sticking out of the glove compartment. He begins humming a tune and laughs.

"One bullet—and poof—the future changes."

He watches as Jasmine slows down suddenly and pulls to a stop. He realizes there is another car behind him. He grimaces.

"Bastard—oh well—one more won't matter."

As a security car corners him he grabs the gun from the glove compartment and waits. Seconds tick by as he watches a security guard come towards him. As the man approaches Silas aims his gun at him and slyly shoots him point-blank. The man topples over as blood pours from a gaping hole in his temple.

"Hope his family has funeral insurance."

He jumps out of the car and runs toward Jasmine. She screams and tries to drive away but it does no good. Silas shoots her at close range and begins laughing. His attention turns to look at the little boy sitting in the passenger side of the car. He laughs loudly as he begins circling. Trevor Bell seems terrified as he looks at his mother lying against the window of the car. Blood trickles from a gunshot wound to her neck. Silas takes another step forward preparing for yet another kill. He looks at his gun.

21

"I don't see what the big deal is about. Byron will think it's really cool that I can see dead people—he'll royally envy me."

Tiffany shoots Niels a cautious look and turns to look at the mirror briefly. They are alone in the room again.

"I thought I made myself clear—you're not to ever tell anyone, especially Byron, of what you saw today or yesterday. No one must know you have the ability see me. You have a gift that most human beings don't have. If you tell people what you can see it won't go over well for you. You'll be teased and ridiculed. Is that what you want—your classmates calling you names?"

Niels seems defiant as he looks at Tiffany.

"How come I can see you?"

Tiffany shrugs and waves her hand in the air.

"I don't know—you just can. Normally someone can only see me if I allow them to. But you're different—special."

Niels angrily points his finger at Tiffany.

"I'm not a freak."

Tiffany takes a step toward Niels and sighs.

"I never said you were a freak."

Page 163

"Are there a lot of you guys hanging around—watching us every day? Waiting for someone to do something stupid?"

Tiffany laughs and wags her finger at Niels. He looks around the room and then faces Tiffany again. He sighs.

"Where did they go?"

Tiffany shrugs her shoulders.

"Do we have an understanding?"

Niels looks at Tiffany curiously and nods.

"I won't tell anyone. I'll pretend it never happened."

Tiffany smiles broadly and seems pleased.

"Can Maxwell Pendergraft see you?"

Tiffany shakes her head.

"Not unless I allow him to."

Niels sighs loudly.

"He's not special?"

Tiffany shakes her head again.

"You're the first person I've come across that can see me without being allowed to. But I'm sure there are others."

Niels digs his hands into the front pockets of his shorts as he glances at the mirror nearby. He gestures with his hand.

"Can you walk through a mirror?"

Tiffany laughs knowingly.

"What do you think?"

Niels stares at the mirror for a few seconds.

"What's on the other side?"

Tiffany gestures knowingly at Niels.

22

Back Street Cafe

"Never a dull moment here in the islands—it seems the kid that got kidnapped managed to escape—quite the story."

Boris Birney rolls his eyes as he looks at John Smythe sitting across from him holding a newspaper in his hand.

"Kid got lucky. End of story."

John seems annoyed and sighs loudly.

Page 164

"Uh-huh—not so much for that girl out by Santa Maria Beach. Some freak strangled her—raped her apparently."

Boris seems about to gag. He takes a sip of coffee from his mug as he bites into a bagel. John notices and grins.

"Boyfriend killed her—no doubt about it."

Boris waves his hand in the air.

"Alison is gonna take that job in Miami."

John reacts and seems upset.

"Tough break—I knew you liked her."

Boris takes another sip of coffee.

"I'm going with her."

They look at each other.

23
Mountain Top

Silas is surrounded by several police officers as he turns to glare at Armand standing about ten feet away. He grimaces.

"This isn't the last time you'll see me. I'm going to get you if it's the last thing I do. Count on it dear brother."

Armand shakes his head as he watches Silas being led toward a waiting police car. He looks at where the covered bodies of Jasmine and the security guard lie. He turns away.

24

Niels looks intently at the mirror for a few seconds as he seems to be expecting something to happen. He sighs.

"She never told me her name."

He looks at his computer.

"Maybe I can scan the drawing and see if anyone knows who she was—she had to be someone—someone recent."

He walks over to where the drawing is lying on his desk and picks it up. Niels smiles as he walks over to the scanner.

"Google knows everything."

He reacts as he looks at the drawing.

"What? What's happening?"

As he stares in shocked amazement the drawing begins to disintegrate in his hand. He reacts. Seconds later he hears laughter and sees Tiffany staring back at him from the mirror.

"I thought I made myself clear."

Niels stands motionless for several seconds as Tiffany waves and then blends back into the mirror until there's nothing there. He turns around and looks at the computer again.

25
Ganz Driveway

"Don't stand here and insult my intelligence thinking I'm going to be impressed by your offer—the answer is no."

Travis looks at Albert Ganz and grimaces.

"This is as good as an offer as you'll ever get. Not a penny more. I won't tolerate money-grubbing trash like you and your daughter running roughshod over my family. The jig is up."

Albert wrings his hand and shrugs.

"I'll see you in court."

Travis angrily clenches his fist.

"I'll destroy you."

Albert rolls his eyes.

"My lawyer will certainly welcome this threat—I hope you have your ducks in a row Nickerson—it would be such a shame if dear Cliff ended up spending the next forty years in jail."

He begins laughing and points at Travis.

"Just imagine what his life will be like in jail after he's convicted for murdering that poor girl—playing peek-a-boo in the shower with some local tough that likes young guys. No doubt he'll see plenty of action—be quite the crowd pleaser."

Travis seems about to explode.

"You'll regret tangling with me Ganz."

Albert waves his hand in the air.

"Have you forgotten who my lawyer is Nickerson? Must I mention the name Carson Penney and his pathetic ending?"

Travis grimaces once more and glances at his car. He faces Albert again and grins broadly. He pulls out his cell phone.

"Heed my warning Ganz—be afraid."

He begins dialing as Albert watches curiously.

26
Blakely Mansion

"I knew this would end badly—told him as much—but did he listen to me—did he heed my warning—of course not."

Savannah Windsor seems nervous as she walks back and forth in her room. She glances at the cell phone lying nearby and sighs loudly. Seconds tick by as she stands motionless while her hands nervously slide through her hair. She sighs again.

"Where is he? Where could he be?"

She walks toward the balcony just as Byron walks into her room. He looks at her curiously for several seconds. He glances at her cell phone lying on the table and is about to reach for it when she turns around and realizes she's no longer alone. He reacts as she shoots him a warning look. He gestures with his hand.

"What's going on with you?"

Savannah grabs her cell phone.

"Nothing is going on me with me."

Byron gives her a knowing look and grins.

"I'm not stupid. I know something is going on that you don't want anyone to know about. Did your boyfriend kick you to the curb? Did he lose interest and find someone else to play with while you're here working? Did he score with some chick he picked up at a sleazy bar and pretend it never happened."

Savannah looks at Byron oddly.

"Have you been watching reruns of *Knots Landing* again? I told you not to watch that show—not until you're older."

Byron rolls his eyes and points at her.

"Don't try to change the subject—did you get dumped by your boyfriend—did he play around on you behind your back?"

Savannah slowly takes a step toward Byron.

"I thought I told you that I didn't have a boyfriend—stop reading more into this than there is—leave me alone."

Byron circles Savannah and smirks.

"Uh-huh—I know something is going on with you. What is it? Are you in some sort of trouble? Are you a drug dealer?"

Savannah turns around to look at Byron.

27
Magens Bay Beach

Omar Cortez shuffles his feet in the sand as he walks along the surf. He looks up every now and then as people walk past him. He nervously glances several times at his cell phone.

"I guess I'm in the clear for killing Ava—the cops busted Cliff for the deed—stupid bastard has no idea it was me. Serves him right after how he's treated everyone on this island."

He stifles a laugh and faces the ocean.

"No way his rich daddy can get him off now—they're gonna throw the book at that moron—will probably get forty years for killing Ava. No amount of money will help him."

He stifles another laugh and smirks.

28

"The plane leaves at ten tonight. Justin is in one of his moods. Made it clear I had to make the flight—no excuses."

Scott reaches out and kisses Sandra.

"That guy is seriously getting on my nerves. He assumes his job gives him the right to make our lives miserable. I think he needs to get to know what my fist feels like across his jaw."

Sandra pretends to slap Scott.

"Don't you even think about hitting him—besides, you're one to talk with Roland Parker constantly ordering you to go after some stupid insane story in order to sell more newspapers."

Scott laughs loudly and sits up in bed.

"I still say I ought to smack Justin around a bit."

Sandra pulls Scott toward her and kisses him.

"Justin has a black belt in Karate."

Scott faces Sandra.

"I'll take my chances."

Sandra slides her fingers across Scott's chest and pushes him back onto the bed. They look at each other. He smirks.

"I'm a troubled dude—deal with it."

Sandra wags her finger at Scott as he laughs.

"Is Manslow really a black belt?"

Sandra nods several times.

"Uh-huh—taught classes for a while."

Scott seems upset.

"He would've deserved a couple of whacks across his jaw. Wipe that perennial smirk off his face—make him humble."

Sandra wags her finger at Scott again.

"Maybe we should start packing before we fall behind and Justin blows his top—gives me one of his boring lectures."

Scott nods in agreement. They laugh.

29
Boston

"Don't you worry about anything Ganz—that idiot is going to find out how hard I can play. His son ending up in the slammer for murder is the least of his worries. It seems according to what my diligent investigators have uncovered in the last two hours or so—Nickerson has been playing fast and loose with paying his taxes. I think he should be made aware I know his secret—add fuel to the fire just to get things moving in our direction."

Jeremy leans back in his chair and grins slyly.

"I'll get him to agree to a settlement quickly or risk yours truly turning him into the IRS. Those brutes are worst than the mob—they have been known to bring grown men to tears before they sacrifice their lives at the end of a gun rather than spend decades in prison for cheating on their taxes. Nickerson certainly will see the benefit of paying what he owes your daughter."

He stands up and walks over to the window.

"Uh-huh—give me a few minutes and I'll give Nickerson a call—give him a dose of things to come. Shake him up a bit."

He begins laughing hysterically as he faces his office again. Jeremy shuts the cell phone off and smiles broadly.

30
Frenchman's Reef Resort

Victoria de Hoya seems annoyed while she walks back and forth as she looks at the screen on her cell phone. Milo Wiley is staring back at her. He doesn't look happy. She sighs loudly.

"I don't know what good it'll do. I barely know her. She and I talked a few times—that's all. I don't see how I can convince Madame Valois to sell her plantation in South Africa to us, especially after what happened between her and Alexander. That woman took it personally when she found out my brother had bedded her eldest daughter—things have never been the same since that day—she swore she'd destroy him—and tried."

Milo runs his fingers through his hair.

"Alexander isn't going to like losing such a lucrative situation—it'll put him in a funk for days—weeks probably."

Victoria rolls her eyes and sighs.

"He'll get over it."

She blows a kiss to Milo and watches as the image on her cell phone fades to black. She shakes her head several times.

"That brother of mine never learns from his mistakes no matter how many times he gets burned—terribly sad."

She walks over to the mini bar just as there is a knock on the door. She walks toward the door seemingly upset. As she opens the door her face wreaths into a huge smile as she sees Maxwell standing there with a single red rose in his hand.

"How about we go out to dinner?"

Victoria grins broadly and pulls Maxwell toward her. They kiss passionately for several minutes. She looks at the rose.

"What happened to Diana Munroe?"

Maxwell makes a flying motion with his hand and grins as Victoria pulls him toward her. She takes the rose from his hand and smells it. They look at each other. Maxwell kisses her.

"I've got a few more days here if you must know. There's this little boy that was kidnapped. Got to follow that through to the end—make sure his kidnapper ends up behind bars."

Victoria seems annoyed and sighs.

"Tonight I just want you to focus on me—focus on what you're going to do to me later—make an impression."

Maxwell gestures with his hand.

31
Mountain Top

Brent Crawford looks out at the city of Charlotte Amalie in a distance. He carefully pulls a baseball cap over his face as he glances at the narrow road leading past several homes. He grits his teeth as he remains silent for a few seconds. He grimaces.

"That miserable little brat is never going to finger me to the cops—I'll kill him first. One clear shot to the head."

He grins broadly as he wipes sweat from his brow.

"When I'm through with that Anderssen kid I'll deal with my sister once and for all—pay her back for selling me out."

Brent starts the engine of his car and sighs.

TO BE CONTINUED

A Brief Look at the Final Episode

Nothing is what it seems as several people encounter events they hadn't anticipated while a little boy experiences a frightening encounter that leaves an impression on him as well as others.

Episode 7
Moments in Time

1
Frenchman's Reef Resort

Maxwell Pendergraft watches as Victoria de Hoya walks toward the restroom. As he turns around he catches a glimpse of a teenage girl standing near the entrance of the fancy restaurant. He reacts as Tiffany Johnson casually walks toward him.

"He's in danger. Go to him."

She points at the door and is gone seconds later.

"Is something wrong Maxwell?"

He turns to see Victoria looking at him.

"I'm sorry. I have to go."

Victoria watches as Maxwell stands up.

"What? Why?"

Maxwell glances at his watch.

"I'll make it up to you. I'm sorry."

He rushes out of the restaurant in a panic. Victoria pulls out her cell phone and looks at it for a few seconds. She sighs.

"That Munroe girl is a real killjoy."

She begins dialing then stops suddenly.

"Diana Munroe. It has to be her. Probably tempted him with a photo of herself in bed without underwear—slut."

She seems annoyed as she sits down at the table and reaches for a menu. Several people look at her curiously.

2
Blakely Mansion

Byron Blakely watches in fascination as a man can be seen climbing over some bushes of the house next door. He rubs his eyes several times as he watches the man make his way across the expansive yard toward the house. He sighs several times.

"What are you doing?"

Byron spins around to see Savannah Windsor looking at him. He remains silent as she walks toward him. She stops.

"I asked you a question."

Byron seems annoyed as he looks at Savannah and turns to look at the house next door. She seems in shock as she watches Brent Crawford make his way up one of the stairs leading to the second floor of the mansion. She gasps. Byron seems confused as she bolts from the room. He sighs loudly.

3
Skyline Drive

An abandoned police car is parked at the side of the road. Two police officers are sitting inside as if taking a break. They are unusually silent. Blood lazily drips unto the pavement. A handcuff lies nearby. Calls go unanswered. Several cars pass without stopping. Two joggers notice the car and cautiously edge toward the rear of the car and once realizing, begin dialing frantically.

4

Maxwell seems in a panic as he drives out of the parking lot of Frenchman's Reef just as Tiffany appears once more.

"I'm sorry about Victoria."

Maxwell reacts as he realizes Tiffany is sitting beside him in the car. He nods as she looks at his cell phone flashing.

"What's going on with the kid?"

Tiffany shoots him a cautious look.

5
Main Street

Silas Bell slowly shuts the door of a car and watches as it drives off. He clenches his fist and suddenly seems enraged.

"That brother of mine better watch his back."

He stifles a laugh as he turns onto a side street. He notices a bar up ahead and seems pleased. He sighs loudly.

"Got to get off this godforsaken island for the time being—lie low—bide my time until I can return—return to even the score—make that son-of-a-bitch pay for slighting me."

He clenches his fist again.

"My half-brother took everything away from me that was rightfully mine. He and that wretched mother of his—caused my father to turn his back on me—neglect his chosen firstborn."

Silas stands at the entrance of the bar.

"Payback is gonna be painful—I guarantee it."

He enters the dimly-lit bar seconds later.

6
Mafolie

Maxwell looks at the driveway ahead and sighs. He turns to look at the passenger seat next to him. There's no one in the car with him. He seems nervous as he slowly opens the door.

7

Multiple police cars blanket the area as the bodies of two fallen officers are carefully placed into a coroner's van nearby.

"I guess we better warn Armand Bell that his brother escaped from our custody—and is armed and dangerous."

From behind him his partner Anissa Verde nods in agreement as she watches the door of the coroner's van being shut. They watch as several other officers seem in shock.

"That dude won't make it off this island alive."

Steve Snell clenches his fist and sighs loudly.

"He'll be used for target practice when we catch him—no trial needed. One direct shot and he's done for. No drama."

Anissa shoots Steve a cautious look.

"Better hope Macron doesn't hear you."

Steve gestures with his hand.

<h2 style="text-align:center">8</h2>

Anderssen Estate

Niels Anderssen is sitting in front of his computer as he hears a thumping sound. He walks to the window and looks out but sees nothing. He turns around and shrugs as he walks back toward his computer. As he is about to sit down a flash of light catches his attention. He turns to see Tiffany staring back at him from the mirror. She snaps her fingers several times. He seems confused as he looks at her just at the door to his bedroom suddenly bursts open and he sees Brent standing in the doorway with an evil grin on his face. In his hand is a butcher knife. Niels reacts as Brent shuts the door and laughs. He points at Niels and makes a slashing gesture with his finger across his neck. Niels slowly begins backing away as he glances at the mirror. Tiffany is nowhere to be seen. Brent takes a step forward and grins.

"Time's up kid. You lose—I win."

Niels looks at the window and sighs. Brent notices.

"Don't even think about it—you'll never make it before I cut you. Face it kid—there's no way out—no way. You're gonna die—die really painfully as I finish you off once and for all."

Niels seems frozen in shock as he watches Brent coming closer to him. He looks at the mirror again. He seems afraid.

<h1 style="text-align:center">Page 176</h1>

"I didn't kill Derek—he fell while he was chasing me on the bluffs. I didn't push him. He slipped and fell onto the rocks."

Brent seems annoyed and shrugs.

"I don't give a fuck about Derek. I didn't like him much anyway. It's you I want—dead children tell no tales. Cops can't find me if you're dead and buried. It's time for you to see if there's any truth to those stories that people tell when they're dying."

Brent takes another step forward.

"How about I answer that question right now?"

Brent reacts and turns around but sees nothing. Niels smiles broadly as he sees Tiffany staring back at him from the mirror. He watches as Brent seems confused. He sighs.

"I'm so gonna enjoy slicing your throat open."

As he takes another step the mirror seems to come alive and begins to shake. Brent notices and reacts in shock. Seconds later the mirror explodes outward sending pieces of jagged shards toward Brent. He falls backwards and begins screaming.

"Stay away from me—leave me alone."

Niels watches in fascination as Brent seems to be in pain from some kind of attack. Niels looks at the mirror again. Tiffany is standing in front of the mirror with a huge smile on her face. Suddenly the door opens and Niels sees Savannah standing in the doorway with a gun in her hand. She looks at him and at Brent lying on the floor seemingly in pain. He notices her and quickly jumps to his feet. Niels glances at where Tiffany was standing seconds earlier but she's gone. Savannah watches as Brent seems amused by the fact she's holding a gun in her hand. She sighs.

"What the fuck are you doing here?"

Savannah glances at where Niels is standing and back at Brent. He clenches his fist and looks at the mirror again. It appears intact once more. He shakes his head and grimaces.

"It ends here today. No more."

Brent laughs as he looks at his sister.

"It ends when I say it ends—not you. You don't tell me what to do sister dearest—you're nothing. You've never been and never will be anything other than a damn whore to me."

Page 177

Savannah seems bothered by the comment and looks at the gun in her hand again. Without warning Brent lunges at Savannah and aggressively tries to wrest the gun away from her but she manages to free herself from his grip as Niels watches the scene playing out in front of him somewhat confused. Tears form in Savannah's eyes as she points the gun at Brent once more.

"I've had it—do you hear me. *I've had it.*"

He begins laughing loudly.

9

Reynolds Estate

Armand Bell reels in shock as he's told about the tragic outcome involving his half-brother and police officers. He runs his fingers through his hair multiple times and nods as several undercover police officers are dispatched around his home.

10

Airport Terminal

Scott Malone looks at his cell phone as he shuts it off. He seems upset and grimaces as Sandra King gestures at him.

"Who were you trying to call?"

He turns to face Sandra and shakes his head.

"Pendergraft must be banging his latest flavor."

Sandra shoots Scott a warning look.

"Victoria de Hoya."

Scott rolls his eyes and glances at the lobby ahead and shrugs. Sandra notices and slides her arm around his waist.

"Do you wish you were still single?"

Scott wags his finger at Sandra and sighs.

"I was calling Pendergraft to let him know I'm gonna whip his ass at tennis next time we meet. Dude's ego is over the top and I intend to take him down a peg or two come next month."

Sandra pulls Scott toward her and smirks.

"What about me? What are you gonna do to me?"

Page **178**

Scott makes a lewd gesture with his finger and kisses her several times. He strokes her cheek and kisses her again.

"I'll be animal when we get back to New York."

Sandra reaches out to kiss Scott again.

"I'll hold you to it."

Scott laughs and notices Boris Birney shaking hands with John Smythe as he stands next to a ticket booth. Alison Gluck hugs John and seems about to cry. John gestures briefly.

11

Savannah looks at the gun in her hand and at Brent's body lying at her feet. Blood oozes from a bullet hole in his forehead as time seems to stand still. As Niels stares at Savannah he notices a black shadow moving toward Brent's body. He turns to look at Tiffany and she nods in agreement. He watches as if mesmerized while the black shadow seems to become more solid. As the claw-like creature hovers over Brent's body loud screams are heard as a mist-like cloud emerges from his dead body and is immediately swallowed up by the claw-like creature. There is eerie silence as Niels turns to look at Tiffany and she nods once more. He turns to face Savannah as the frightened woman begins to cry loudly. She begins repeating several times that Brent was her stepbrother. Amid tears she blurts out he had been brutally raping her since she was sixteen—that he ruined her life and forced her to do vile things. Niels seems in shock as she details the abuse she suffered at his hands. Niels continues to stand there unable to move as the cloud-like mist dissipates and he's alone in the room again. Several seconds later he sees Astrid Blakely standing in the doorway with several police officers.

12
Nickerson Mansion

"What do I pay you for? Figure this mess out and get back to me. Winterfield is behind it—that jerk is playing dirty."

Travis Nickerson runs his fingers through his hair as he looks at the computer screen. He grimaces as he notices the look on the face of his lawyer. Wilson Aames seems slightly annoyed as he stares back at Travis from his office. He sighs loudly.

"I already told you I'm aware of what Winterfield is doing to get under your skin by giving Albert Ganz ammunition to use against you. How about you let me enjoy the rest of my day and I'll get back to you first thing in the morning. In the meantime I think you should face reality concerning your troubled son and that dead girl. It doesn't look good—terrible actually. Unless a witness comes forth Cliff could spend the next forty years in jail for murder—and I don't have to tell you what happens to young men in prison that look like a fitness model—he'll be treated like a very delicious lollipop and sampled often by other inmates."

Wilson seems almost gleeful as he graphically details what could befall Cliff if he's sent to prison. Travis reacts and sighs.

13

Maxwell looks at Niels and still seems in shock while he recounts what happened to a police officer. He notices Valerie Anderssen talking with Savannah in the hallway and looks over to where Astrid is standing. She has a curious look on her face.

14

John waves as he watches Boris and Alison walk toward the boarding area several feet away. Seconds later a large monitor positioned on the wall nearby suddenly comes to life as local news crews begin reporting about Brent Crawford and his illicit relationship with his stepsister. He turns away in disgust.

15

"I'm so sorry. I had no idea that your stepbrother was still alive. I assumed he died in the fire that killed your mother."

Savannah wipes tears from her eyes as Astrid hugs her warmly. They look at each other for a few seconds. In a distance Maxwell is standing next to Niels and Valerie. As Maxwell turns he sees Tiffany standing on the other side of the mirror. She waves to him and then is gone. Maxwell sighs loudly and faces Niels.

Several Hours Later

16
Anderssen Estate

"Are you going to be all right?"

Maxwell seems worried as he watches Niels looking out the window. He remains silent for a second or two and then turns to face Maxwell. He takes a step forward then stops.

"Do you think they'll make what happened to me into a movie? Get some famous child star to play me on the screen."

Maxwell stifles a laugh.

"You were almost killed and all you can think about is whether or not a movie will be made about what just happened to you? Aren't you the least bit freaked out about anything?"

Niels gestures with his hand.

"Brent Crawford was outgunned."

He looks at the mirror.

"I wasn't alone."

He grins broadly.

"That girl was here."

He turns to look at the mirror again and sighs.

"She warned me."

Maxwell looks at the mirror.

"Who are you talking about? What girl?"

Niels comes toward Maxwell. He seems annoyed.

"How dumb do you think I am? You knew all along that girl I saw at Mandahl Beach was a ghost. I could tell by the way you were acting—almost like you were trying to protect her."

Maxwell looks at the cell phone in his hand.

"There are just things you don't understand."

Niels looks at the mirror again.

"I understand more than you think. I've read a lot of books on paranormal encounters. I know what's real and what isn't."

They stare at each other for a few seconds.

"What's her name? What happened to her? How did she die? How do you know her? How long have you known her?"

Maxwell slowly runs his fingers through his hair. He seems in shock at the barrage of questions. Niels comes closer.

"Do you know or don't you?"

Maxwell looks at his cell phone again.

"There are things that exist. I really don't think you need to know what is and what isn't. Leave it alone. Forget what took place at Mandahl. Forget anything ever happened at that beach. Certain things are best left unanswered. When you're older you'll understand. Right now you just need to be a kid. Enjoy life."

Niels looks at Maxwell and then at the door. He walks toward the door and locks it. He turns to face Maxwell.

"You're not leaving until you tell me."

Maxwell looks at Niels standing defiantly at the door. He sighs loudly. He glances at his watch. He shuffles his feet.

"I can't tell you. Can't you understand that? There are just certain things that are not supposed to be talked about."

"How come I can see her and not you?"

Maxwell runs his fingers through his hair again.

"I have no idea."

"That's not an answer."

They stare at each other for a few seconds.

"Who was she? What's her name?"

Maxwell shakes his head and grimaces.

"I think it's time for me to leave."

Niels notices Maxwell looking at his cell phone again and seems upset. He suddenly lunges toward Maxwell and grabs the cell phone. He angrily throws it on his bed. Maxwell reacts.

"What the fuck."

They look at each other.

17
Back Street

A couple is walking along the street as shadows seem to hide the whereabouts of other pedestrians walking by.

"This was such a wonderful vacation. Too bad it has to end in a few hours at the airport. Back to Indiana we go."

Casey Wilkersonne smiles as he looks at his wife. She nods in agreement and kisses her husband. There is a sound behind them. As they turn around Casey is hit over the head. Veronica Wilkersonne seems in shock as a man demands her purse after taking her husband's wallet from his limp body. She hesitates.

"Your purse or your life—you decide."

Veronica realizes at that moment the man has a gun. As seconds tick by he seems to become more impatient.

"You have one minute."

She watches as her assailant angrily grabs her purse and disappears through a maze of handicraft stores seconds later.

18
Police Station

"I didn't kill her. I already told you that."

Cliff Nickerson paces back and forth inside a small room as Carl Wyndfeldt-Schmidt taps his fingers on a table nearby.

"We found your semen in her vagina. She was bruised and beaten. Obviously something happened between you two."

Cliff stops and glares at Carl.

"Of course something sexual happened between us. She and I were friends with benefits. Perhaps you've heard of it."

Carl stands. Cliff watches him curiously.

"Why aren't you guys looking for the real killer? Ava Fontaine had plenty of enemies. She pissed off everyone."

Cliff begins laughing loudly. Carl shoots Cliff a look of irritation as he runs his fingers through his hair. Cliff smirks.

Page **183**

"Have you spoken to Lindsay Ganz? What about Bryce and Greg Forbes? They were both screwing her. So was a creep named Omar Cortez—he's enrolled at the University of the Virgin Islands. That dude is a piece of work no doubt. Likes to film sexual encounters with his dumb conquests—then sells the video."

Carl suddenly seems interested in what Cliff is saying. He motions several times for Cliff to sit at the table again.

"What was his name again? Spell it out."

Cliff seems pleased with the turn of events and glances at the door. He gestures at Carl as he sits down. He sighs loudly.

19
Television Station

Curtis Marlowe shuts off his cell phone and looks at his older sister. He seems bothered by something. Jennifer Marlowe notices her brother's demeanor. She glances at the cell phone.

"This just happened?"

Curtis shakes his head and stands up.

"Uh-huh—they're at the police station as we speak."

Jennifer gestures with her hand.

"I'll call Shelby and tell her to meet you."

Curtis grabs his jacket.

"I'm on my way. Five minutes at the latest."

Jennifer watches him leave. She slowly turns to look at the computer screen and reacts. She seems bothered and sighs.

20
Airplane

"Is Justin on the plane with us? I didn't see him earlier when we boarded. He seemed preoccupied at the signing."

Sandra turns to look at Scott and smiles.

"He's gonna take the next flight. I told him we needed to be alone—got something to talk to you about—important."

Scott nervously wrings his hands several times.

Page 184

"I told you already—I wasn't trying to score with that reporter. I've been nothing if not a wonderful husband."

Sandra takes Scott's hand in hers and smiles.

"This is something else completely."

She leans over and kisses him. He kisses her back.

"I'm going to need you more than I've ever needed you before once we get back to the mainland. Roland is not going to like it one bit—but you'll have to curtail your work schedule."

Scott looks at Sandra curiously.

"Is something wrong? Are you all right?"

Sandra reaches out to gently stroke Scott's face.

"My mother has gotten her wish."

Scott looks at Sandra and seems confused.

"What's that supposed to mean?"

Sandra takes Scott's hand and places it on her stomach as he continues looking at her seemingly confused. She sighs.

"How does becoming a father sound to you?"

Scott reacts. He looks at Sandra.

21
Market Square

"It was just a matter of time before Cliff Nickerson got busted for something heinous. It doesn't surprise me one bit."

June McQueen shakes her head several times.

"He got what he deserved. Good riddance."

Wendy Crowe seems upset at June's remark and glances at the front door. June notices and grabs her arm.

"I'm sorry. I knew you and Cliff were quite close."

Wendy waves her hand in the air.

"We were. I didn't think Cliff was capable of something like that. He and I have known each other since second grade."

She looks at her cell phone lying nearby.

"I thought he and Ava were tight. I guess I was wrong. Isabel Black is probably breathing a sigh of relief right now."

She glances at the entrance again.

"Cliff hated her—made threats. I expected."

June takes a sip of her iced coffee.

"You expected Cliff Nickerson to murder Isabel?"

Wendy notices several people seem to be listening from adjoining tables nearby. She faces June again and whispers.

"Of course not—he just wanted to ruin her reputation by taking her virginity. It wasn't a big secret. He told everyone."

Wendy seems pleased with herself.

"He wanted to destroy her for how she treated him. Told me it would be perfect if after he fucked her she became pregnant—had to face getting an abortion—said he would enjoy watching her being humiliated—shamed for her behavior."

Wendy makes a lewd gesture with her finger.

"I didn't see anything wrong with what he wanted to do to her. Isabel Black is a snob—behaves like she's perfect."

June rolls her eyes and turns away.

"She was always nice to me. She was never rude."

Wendy gives June a nasty look.

"That's because you're not in her social circle of theater people. She probably doesn't even know who you are."

June seems disgusted and reacts.

"At least I'm not facing murder charges."

She smiles broadly seeing Wendy's discomfort.

"I wonder what Lindsay Ganz is going to do now? I assume she'll have no problem getting her hands on Cliff's money."

Wendy shrugs as several people walk by.

Two Days Later

22

Airport Terminal

"When will I see you again—enjoy your company?"

Maxwell laughs as Victoria playfully tugs at the buttons on his Levi's. He wags his finger at her and smirks broadly.

"I've got some free time next month."

Page **186**

Victoria makes a lewd gesture with her finger and they hug warmly as he turns to look at several people walking by.

"I'll hold you to your word—count on it."

Maxwell laughs loudly and hugs Victoria again.

"You'll be the death of me no doubt."

Victoria winks and licks her lips. She notices his erection straining under his Levi's. She gives him a knowing look.

"Would that be so bad?"

Maxwell looks at Victoria and grins.

"I've got plenty of game left in me yet."

Victoria slides her hand over his erection and smiles. She kisses him lightly and then more passionately. She sighs.

"I'm thinking of booking an African safari next year. You'll be my guest of course. Show me your dangerous side when we're alone with nothing but savage wilderness around us for miles."

She pulls him toward her.

"There's just something about you Maxwell. You know how to make women feel special. I'm never bored when you're in my company. Being with you in Africa would be wonderful."

Maxwell leers at Victoria and grins broadly.

"I'll have to check my schedule."

Victoria seems upset.

23
Anderssen Estate

Niels is sitting in front of a computer and reacts as he looks at a photograph of Tiffany Johnson from an old newspaper clipping featured on an online public library. He glances at the headlines and slowly leans back in his chair. He sighs loudly.

About the Series Creator

Gary Brin was born in 1965 and has lived in the United States Virgin Islands, Hawaii and California. He has edited numerous original literary works over the years—both new and revised. In 2019 he established Standish Press to bring forth interesting fictional and historical material usually ignored by mainstream publishers because of specific views or content. In addition to publishing books, he also created the Nancy Hanks Lincoln Public Library (named after the mother of Abraham Lincoln) in 2014 to make available hard-to-find books to a worldwide audience.

Production Notes

Written by Wesley Adams and Daphne McGee
Manuscript edited by Gary Brin
Cover photograph from Adobe Stock Images
Front cover design and interior book layout by Gary Brin
Cover layout by Victoria Valentine
Additional help provided by Carlton J. Young
Series created by Gary Brin

Character List

Wilson Aames
Niels Anderssen
Valerie Anderssen
Viktor Anderssen
Gavin Ayers
Armand Bell
Silas Bell
Trevor Bell
Boris Birney
Hadley Black
Isabel Black
Astrid Blakely
Byron Blakely
Ward Brady
Omar Cortez
Cassandra Covington
Brent Crawford
Norma Crowe
Wendy Crowe
Alexander de Hoya
Alexis de Hoya
Ingrid de Hoya
Victoria de Hoya
Caleb Farrow
Ava Fontaine
Bryce Forbes
Greg Forbes
Albert Ganz
Lindsay Ganz
Abigail Gluck
Alison Gluck
Pamela Henderson

Marla Jefferson
Tiffany Johnson
Sandra King
Shirley Lindstrom
Larisa Lopez
Antonio Macron
Wesley Madison
Scott Malone
Justin Manslow
Curtis Marlowe
Jennifer Marlowe
Jordan McKinney
June McQueen
Diana Munroe
Cliff Nickerson
Travis Nickerson
Roland Parker
Maxwell Pendergraft
Allegra Penn
Maggie Rios
Lane Rolfe
Colin Rossmore
Jasmine Rossmore
Marisa Rossmore
Greg Sharpe
William Sharpe
John Smythe
Steve Snell
Lily Van Tassel
Casey Tyverton
Anissa Verde
Marco Verde
Derek Ving
Milo Wiley
Casey Wilkersonne
Veronica Wilkersonne
Shelby Wilkins
Whitney Wilkins

Savannah Windsor
Jeremy Winterfield
Carl Wyndfeldt-Schmidt
Peter Zimmerman

**Real People, Real
Animals, and Historical
Events Mentioned**

Bob the Cat
Chase Vaults of Barbados
Dorcas Chase
Christina Crawford
Bing Crosby
Bette Davis
Francis Drake
Anne Frank
Tom Holland
Barbara Hutton
John F. Kennedy Jr.
Abraham Lincoln
Margaret Mitchell
Michael Phelps
Pocahontas
Princess Diana
Princess Stephanie
Brooke Shields
Robert Wagner
Natalie Wood
F. W. Woolworth
Orville Wright
Wilbur Wright

Last in the Series
Book 10
Return Engagement

Standish Press

www.ingramcontent.com/pod-product-compliance
Lightning Source LLC
Chambersburg PA
CBHW061307210726
48293CB00003B/1153